I0775510

BURNOUT

BURNOUT

THE BURNER TRILOGY
BOOK THREE

MARIANNA PALMER

Red Empress Publishing
www.RedEmpressPublishing.com

Copyright © Marianna Palmer

Cover Design by Cherith Vaughan
https://www.facebook.com/coversbycherith

All rights reserved. No part of this publication may be reproduced, stored in a retrieval system, or transmitted in any form or by any means, electronic, mechanical, photocopying, recoding, or otherwise, without the prior written consent of the author.

PROLOGUE

REDMOND

*L*aoni, we have to go.

We're leaving you. I can't believe this. It's the worst thing I've ever done. But I gotta get your family to safety. I gotta get our friends out.

I hate myself! I'm choosing them over you.

But Natalie tells me we'll draw their fire away if we leave. You can't come with us.

You're still in that Burner Augmenter. If we take you out now, you'll die. If we don't leave, we'll all die. And thanks to my stinking trace...

I can't stay with you, or I'll lead them right to you.

They're coming.

Find this, Laoni. Find us.

Find me.

I'll always love you.

Redmond.

CHAPTER 1

I lived in dreams. I knew they were dreams. My life never worked out like this. I wandered through amusement parks. Not like the times when I was attacked. Ones where Mond and I went on rides, enjoyed cotton candy, laughed at each other's jokes. Like a real date.

Then it'd change. But what amazed me was that I was always happy. No nightmares. No Riders. No Breathers. No danger. Just me and my guy, holding each other.

I felt weak at first in my dreams. Only walking. Never wearing more than the barest minimum of clothing. Then it grew more elaborate—coats, vests, long pants.

Logic couldn't find me in the sleep of dreams, but I knew I was growing stronger. That's why the change in not only attire but also location. The scenarios became more vivid.

Redmond always walked alongside me, giving me that special grin. That look that told me I was the only girl for him.

Then it changed.

Redmond was gone. Fire filled my sky. I walked endless

paths with ugly gray roads. I still walked in a peaceful world, but I was alone. Where was he? Where was I?

Dreams always end.

My eyes flashed open to liquid. My nose felt full. I was drowning!

My heart pulsed through my neck and I started thrashing. Reality was coming back to me.

I had air. A round breathing thing around my nose. I settled down and tried to get my bearings. The last thing I could remember was attacking Molly in her suit. Killing her.

I had been killing myself too.

But I was alive!

A thrill went through me. I was still here! I hadn't died.

But... I blinked, trying to see through the liquid around me. All I saw was glass. Beyond that, my vision was too warped to see what it was. All I saw was a whole lot of...

No. I couldn't see. I felt for my electricity, the stuff that had been draining me and found...

Ice! I reached out and froze the liquid around me, making a spear. I wondered why the whole thing wasn't a frozen cube around me. But my mind was in fragments. Still halfway caught up in the dream where Mond left. Where was he now?

I threw out my hand and ice met glass.

Water I hadn't frozen went everywhere. I flowed with it. The oxygen was ripped off my nose and I landed. My hair fell around me. White again. I lovingly stroked every strand. I was back. I was alive!

I didn't look around. I just threw my ice. A tiger here... icy teeth and claws, darkened stripes with black ice. A moon and stars slowly floating through chilled air. I was more than back. I was...bringing ice at my behest. There was plenty of liquid to work with, but I was making it exist. I walked without looking where I was going.

I ignored the chaos around me. The fact that no one was around. No one waited, ready to greet me. No Redmond.

The air was chilly. The sky finally greeted me. It was slate gray, a glowing orange behind it, obscured as if it would snow. But I felt no moisture in the air.

I finished my ice sculptures. I made a chair and sunk into it, looking at my perfectly preserved dress. All the water on it was still dripping. I quickly froze it. I had changed. This dress was not made of the clothing Natalie gave me, the stuff she had somehow made to prevent Burners' powers from going out of control. Yet, I sat here like I was normal. I controlled anything that froze. It didn't just happen.

I was back more than I ever was before.

But a gnawing worry dug into my backbone. I finally asked the most important question.

What happened?

Death had been so close. I had looked him in the eye and then said goodbye. I had gone backward on that long dark tunnel, away from the light. But...was I really here? Anywhere?

If I was alive, where was Mond? Where were my friends? Erin with her pessimism? Cindy with her devotion? Natalie with her leadership?

Even Rust Smythe, the alien living on Earth, would have been welcome. But no one was here.

Was I really dead after all?

Somehow, I didn't think so. I felt. I was here. I was uncomfortable. I was hungry. How could you be hungry in the afterlife? And if this was the afterlife, then why did it look so...real?

Finally, I was able to clear my eyes. To accept what was around me.

Ruins. Rubble as far as the eye could see. Nothing and nobody alive. I was in the remains of a city. New York, but I only knew it by memory. There was nothing left to give any sign of recognition. I was in a wasteland. Everything was devastated.

My joy was leaking out, air in a punctured balloon. I should have known! Joy never lasts long with me.

I heard a low hum, the sound of an engine overhead.

I stood and looked into the sky, my hair fluttering in a sick breeze. The sound was made not by natural means but by a ship that flew overhead. The dust around me picked up and reached my nose. I tried to keep down the urge to cough.

The ship was familiar to me. At least it looked like a place I had been in before. The Riders' ship.

This was definitely not an afterlife. It was after life. After my life had ended. I didn't even know *when* I was, but I knew this wasn't my death.

It was my future. Now, my present.

The ship glimmered, reflecting the gray and dust around me. It hovered there. A red, round beam suddenly bubbled over the top of the silver dome and rolled down.

"Cover this area with an ice shield!" a voice hissed.

Proving how much I was used to danger, I listened without hesitation. I quickly touched my hands together and broke them apart, pushing a shield above me and the mysterious voice just as the red beam poured over us. It vibrated, moaned like a dying animal, but then it retreated and the ship flew on.

I looked toward my elbow and saw an old man. He wore something very strange. A one-piece robe with a cloak... thing. It looked like it was made out of fire, but it didn't burn or melt anything near me.

"What happened?" I asked. Or I thought I did. My vocal cords were out of practice. I hummed and moaned.

"It's okay. I think I know what you're going to ask. Just keep trying. Your voice will return. Burners are quick healers. But I'll answer your moaned question. Ice, or fire, blocks their scans. That red beam would have seen you and then picked you up. But you blocked it. This fire cloak protects me, but you would have been discovered had you not used the shield."

I pointed to him and moaned some more. "Who…" was all I got out.

"You don't remember your old doctor?" he asked with a grin.

Memories flooded in. Rust Smythe. But he was not…

"It's been a very long time, Laoni." The wrinkles on his face multiplied as he grinned. I couldn't function. Math started pouring into my head. He had been forty, at most. Now he was…

"One hundred and forty-five. It's been more than one hundred years." He flipped his cloak. Then he laughed. "Sorry for the dramatics. The cloak made me do it."

I whimpered.

"Oh, the cloak? Some technology mixed with Burner skills. Helped into existence by me and…"

I flailed my hands and he stopped talking. I had to get this out. I couldn't have Rust Smythe misinterpret my questions anymore. "Where…is…Redmond?"

A hundred years zinged inside my head. But Rust was still alive. Mond couldn't be…

"Burners live long, but not that long. He died some years after the invasion."

My world was gone. My mind crumpled around me like the ruins. I knew I had come back to rubble. But he was supposed to still exist somewhere in this world. He wasn't dead!

"Come on. I've got a fire fortress not far from here. It will help."

"Kill…me," I said. Tears were streaming down my face. Not ice. Water. Annoying, trickling water. I gestured and they became ice balls. "I… don't…want to live. I don't want to fight whatever that is. Just kill me. Please." My voice came back in a wail.

"Oops, I buried the lead. There's a way to save him. So, no, I won't kill you." Rust grabbed a hold of my hand. "Please, let's go. Your ice shield is faltering. They have ships fly over every so often."

"Why?" I asked, but let him lead me. I had died with the news that Mond was dead. I was reborn when Rust said I could save him. But I could barely breathe or think. So much had hit me. I didn't know how I was still standing…or walking. "The world is destroyed."

"This city is," Rust corrected. "But the Riders—as you know them—or the Imposters—as I do—have made new cities that fit into their world. They have found themselves a new home. It's like a giant hive. You know where New Mexico used to be?"

I blinked. "No." I was never good at geography.

"Well, let's just say all roads lead to Albuquerque now. The whole state has become a prison for humans with a giant breeding ground for Riders."

We climbed and crawled over rubble until I saw a fiery mound rising above everything else. The rubble of lots of buildings met an invisible wall where everything near it burned. Rust pulled out a weapon—or it looked like a weapon, but it was something that pushed a blue beam out in front of us and cleared a path so we could walk toward the fire fortress.

It was so beautiful. Red and glowing against all the gray

around. I would have expected to smell smoke with all that fire, but only a pleasant aroma reached me.

"What about Breathers? Flyers?" I asked, still not fully functioning.

Rust sighed and pushed his hood down to reveal a mane of light green hair. He laughed as I stared. "Hey, humans get gray when they get old; we Simrulians get green. Young, we look like Earthers, but old, we look…different."

I could see that. The freckles that I once noticed had grown into moon-shaped curves all the way down his neck and up his chin.

"To answer your question. No, they weren't needed anymore. Breathers died out. Flyers were terminated."

I shuddered. His tone had gotten serious. There was no way the Flyers just died in battle. They were executed. "So, only Riders…the Imposters are left?"

Rust put his weapon away and pulled out what looked like a television remote. He pushed a few buttons and a whole wall opened, the fire flickering down to nothing. We walked in under the domed archway into a metal world. The door closed behind us and Rust led me up a ramp into what looked like a living room. He gestured to a couch and I sunk into it. My dress bunched under me and I questioned my wisdom about wearing this thing.

"Rust…what happened?"

He shook his head and walked over to a black box on which he pushed a few buttons. Seconds later, the smell of roast beef filled my nostrils and he pulled out a fully made Reuben sandwich and handed it over. I practically attacked it.

It tasted…good! Not frozen. Not empty. Just like bread and meat, squished together with dressing and sharp sauerkraut. The same box dinged a second later and he handed over a cherry soda.

I forgot everything. It was all so…foreign. But eating, drinking, just feeling my energy restored by what my body didn't reject. I fell into a food-induced stupor, just relishing it.

All too soon, I had to come back to normal. To face what was out there. To fight again. That was my life.

CHAPTER 2

I took my time finishing my food, holding off the conversation I'd have to have as long as possible.

"Okay," I finally said, looking around for a sink to put my dishes into. Rust surprised me and just pushed it back into that same black box. "Like Star Trek?" I asked.

Rust smiled. "Redmond loved the idea of a food replicator."

Sadness overtook me. I shook my head to clear it. Mond wasn't dead. At least Rust said I could save him. "And this building…it's his too, isn't it?"

Rust sat down and shrugged his cloak off. He put his hands behind his head, and I saw what looked like gills down his arms. "Yes. The cloak as well. He didn't know what to do with himself without you. He used to be destructive, but when I told him it was better to channel it into what you'd want him to do, he started creating. He made a lot of inventions that helped."

I couldn't speak. I knew that whatever Mond had done, it hadn't been enough. "You said we could save him? How? When did he die? What age?"

"I think he lasted until forty. He couldn't live a lifetime without you. He had no faith left in our vision."

I closed my eyes. Mond had died. He wasn't alive. I didn't think I'd make it to forty, either. Wait...

"How old am I? Do I have wrinkles? Am I an old woman?" I hadn't seen myself in a mirror since I woke up.

Rust hid a grin. "Teenagers," he whispered. But before I could take offense, he added, "You were unageing in the machine. No cells died. Nothing changed. You are still seventeen."

Still seventeen...after a hundred years. Incredible. But no more than what had already happened. I stretched my legs out, looking at the mounds of material on top of them. I had worn this dress to my death, and it had been interrupted. Then I had gone to my death again and been saved.

But while I slept, my world had died. "What happened?" My question was getting redundant, but Rust hadn't answered it.

"Invasion," he said. He gazed off into space, reliving old memories. An old guy caught up in the past. "About a year after we put you into the machine and you started showing signs of coming back, a ship attacked. More than one, actually. All over the world. They shot through the sky. On the surface, the army of Breathers attacked. They didn't kill. They captured.

"We tried to stop them, but they headed for the major cities first. To get rid of the majority of the population. They didn't need a lot of humans. Just enough to... Well, you remember the Riders' ship. The newborns."

I did. Those gaping mouths of goop haunted the furthest recesses of my brain. The baby skin they were melding into. "So, the survivors became Riders."

"Young and old," Rust affirmed. He was remembering

two times. One where his world was lost, and one where mine was. "Riders..."

"Imposters," I corrected. "I like that term better. It's more accurate."

Rust inclined his head. "Okay. The Imposters prefer babies because they can be nurtured from the beginning. But with their system, any human can become their new... Let's say host. But there's not much left of the original person."

I put my chin in my hand. "The Breathers were their handiwork, huh? And I thought we had done some good."

Rust waved his hands in the air desperately. "You did. But you also pushed the invasion along. Molly was kind of their contact. She kept them at bay, promising willing slaves if they just marketed it right. So, La'R-Gon, the...what you'd call emperor, stayed put, waiting somewhere out there." Rust gestured to the ceiling, but it was far above in the stars he was referring to.

"But with Molly's death, with the breeding grounds destroyed, he launched his attack. Breathers showed up. The horned ones. The teethed ones."

My eyes felt too big. "The *what?*"

Rust gave an old smile, surrounded by wrinkles. "Oh, yeah. You weren't aware of the other experiments they did. The things I was fighting my whole life."

He closed his eyes and leaned back. I saw a weariness that I never had before. Whatever I could have said about Rust before, he was never *tired*. But he was now.

"What are those things?" I wasn't ready to think too hard. Get answers, that's all.

"Breathers were made to combat what my parents created. The Imposters did experiments on DNA and tried to connect them. That was what Bru'G-un decided to copy— the use of your natural elements as a weapon. But Molly Larson was hard to satisfy. She told Bru'G-un to put forth to the emperor that other things on Earth might help in an invasion—more, they'd help to convince the normal people that they'd love to have a slaver if they could acquire new abilities. A campaign to make people desire a new leader."

It was all so confusing. My head spun, trying to take it all in. "You mean, if they let the Imposters come in, steal our bodies, they'd become, like, um, vampires?"

Rust laughed. "Kind of. Werewolves, vampires, extra abilities. Things like that. Not in the mythical sense, of course. DNA connection."

My mouth dried out before I could close it. "Those things exist?"

Rust sighed. "Not anymore. They were a lark. Good for the invasion, but gone quickly. The only things existing now are humans that become bodies for the Imposters. They already number past the billions. They'll have to send some out to other planets if they keep growing."

I clenched my fists a few times. Billions! "Is that what happened to your planet?"

Rust gave a small smile. "No. We destroyed our planet rather than let them have it. It's in pieces now."

Black acid oozed throughout my body. "And that's the only way to save this one, isn't it? You want me to destroy it."

To my surprise, Rust laughed. "No!"

I had always disliked his sense of humor. "There are billions out there!" I snapped and stood up. "Mond is gone. And…"

Rust sobered up. "Yes. All of them are dead. All the people you knew. And they didn't die of old age," he said meaningfully.

"You are a jackass!" I exploded. "You survive? For what? To always run and hide? To remember the people you betrayed by living while they died? I don't get this! Why did I live? Why was my machine not destroyed? I would have liked it better to wake up dead!"

Rust hid a smile. "Yes, probably. But to answer your rather rude questions… First, your machine was protected by an energy not easily penetrated. I think it has something to do with the Burner powers it controlled. Only a direct elemental attack could destroy it, which you did. Second, I survived for only one reason. Otherwise, I would have killed myself long ago. I know an easy death for my kind."

I didn't calm down. I walked over to a sizeable fiery window and stared out at the destruction. The vast empty landscape did nothing for my mood.

"Third, we can save them all. The Earth. Everything."

My head snapped as I spun it to look at him. "They are all dead! How can we save the dead?"

"By stopping them from dying in the first place."

I swallowed three times, trying to get the ball of pain out of my throat. "We could do that?"

"Time travel, baby," Rust said with a grin. He let out a manic cackle, and I wondered, not for the first time, if I was dealing with a sane man.

"Time travel? Okay, I know a science fiction novel is happening around us, but that goes a bit too far, doesn't it?"

Rust surprised me with a snarl. "No. I'm quite serious. Redmond believed in it too."

A wave of sadness took me over. Of course Mond would believe in it. He loved all those kinds of things. "But time is just a concept made up by humans. The sun goes around, but that's the only thing that marks time. The year could be 900 still, if not changed by our reckoning. Or 65 million or so. Whatever."

Rust jumped up and made a timeout symbol with his hands. "Pessimism is a defensive mechanism for those who are afraid to hope. Don't be scared."

But I was. Everything had gone so wrong. I just wanted to curl up in a ball and end my existence. Not worry anymore. Not think. Not try...

"You can have it all. Look..." He plinked a button on the wall, and an interactive screen dropped down from the ceiling. He put in a strange password, and lots of files came up. He opened a drawing program and drew a line down the screen. "Time is an entity just like ice or fire or lightning. It lives and breathes. It...moves."

I tried not to laugh. "Ice is alive? Fire?"

"Shut your trap," Rust said kindly. "There's a force out there that goes beyond my understanding, beyond even the Imposters'. It exists beyond our plane of existence. See this line. Let's just say it is our time. Here..."

He drew a squiggly line halfway down the line. "This is where everything went wrong." He pushed the rest of the line, and it became squiggly too. "Like a rock thrown in a pond, the ripples showed its effect. If you could stop that..."

He undid his action, and the line went back to straight.

"But..." Logic was going crazy. "If I did, wouldn't it already be done? I mean, wouldn't we not be having this conversation? I wouldn't even be in the machine anymore."

Rust clapped his hands together. "Wrong! You are thinking of time as linear. That if you did something in the past, it would already be done. We're talking about cause and effect here. The effect doesn't happen before the cause. It's not possible. Time is not linear. It is a beast that moves when it's affected. If you could talk to the entity, you could travel on its back toward the past and see about changing it. Once you did, the line would snap back in place, just like it did when I undid my progress. It's that simple."

I stared at him, my mouth hanging open again. "Is it?"

"Doing it, yes. Getting in contact with the entity, no."

I slipped back to the couch and hid my eyes. Hope was

warring with despair. Rust was right. Believing it wouldn't work was easier than actually trying. "What do we have to do?"

Rust laughed and clapped his hands. "Redmond and I and Natalie, of course, before she died, were working on a telepathic communication device. Not unlike the one that controls the Breathers."

I groaned loudly. "Like what? What are you talking about? The Flyers?"

Rust bared his teeth. "No! Oh, right. You aren't aware. Look, we found something out after the whole thing with Molly. You ever wonder why Breathers were born so evil, with one intent in their minds?"

"Because they're monsters," I shot back.

"They are, but it was because they were programmed to be so right from birth. Molly had so much hatred."

I shook my head. "What?"

Rust gestured for me to walk with him. We headed out of the living room and down one very long hallway. I was amazed the fiery mess outside didn't heat up the area. It didn't come inside. Mond was amazing.

The hallway was at least a thousand feet long, and at the end there was an open, welcoming area with soft walls and a lounge chair with a clear helmet-like thing complete with a clear face mask, shaped like a face, of course. Mond's face. He had been the mold for it.

"Breathers are machines, Laoni. They are living machines. Programmed with the hatred of the creator. Molly had so much evil in her. She like the idea of powerful creatures laying waste to any Burner in every way possible. She made the minds."

I wanted to scoff. But it all made sense. The evil in the Breathers. All the same exact kind. "And Drake?"

"A misfire in the communication. Drake told me that

when he was being born, something attacked the grounds, and he woke up with no preconceived notions. He chose for himself what was right and what was wrong."

"He's dead. So are Gem and Mom," I said dully.

"Now you're getting it!" Rust exclaimed. "Everyone's dead."

Rust was getting on my nerves. "So, what is this?" I asked, gesturing to the machine.

"Well, like I said. The same thing that controls the Breathers, that gets the evil thoughts into them in the first place, was a great template for us. We used it to try to interrupt the evil made in the minds of our enemies. Instead..." Rust quieted.

His voice was shaded with awe when he said the next sentence. "We encountered a creature that was made of time, or controlled time, or whatever. There was a brief conversation. Mond talked for about two seconds. When he was done, he stared at me and said, 'We can fix it. We can change it all.' So, here we are."

My heart thumped painfully, reminding me how long it had been since I had held Mond. Since I had seen him. "Why couldn't he fix it then?"

"Because his mind couldn't take it. No one could. We all went slightly insane after every attempt. We knew a prolonged connection with the beast would kill us. So, there is only one person who could."

I knew where he was going with this. "Me?"

"Laoni, you've been in that machine for a hundred years, being strengthened. Before that, you had the ultimate Burner powers at your fingertips. If anyone can deal with this, it's you."

I looked at the machine. The mask that presumably went over my face. Mond's over mine. "So, what?"

"The plans I have been agonizing over for years and

years. Step one, get in contact with time itself. Step two, ask for a favor. Step three, go back in time and stop the invasion. Simple." He smiled and crossed his arms.

How could anyone's face be so damned slappable? "You're missing a key point. How do I stop an invasion that my friends couldn't? That even your people couldn't?"

Rust slapped his forehead. "I buried the lead again, didn't I? Come here." He pulled down another screen. This time it showed just blue flashing dots.

"Um, what are they?"

"Proof of a transmission. My parents', to be exact. They knew where the ships were. Maybe how to bring them down."

This sounded good!

"You know how my parents died and made Burners, right? Well, in the same transmission, they sent information to Burners about the location of the ships. We can determine how to take them down if we know where they are. In the subconscious of you, of your friends, is secret data that will, when put together properly, give you all the information you need to take them down."

Okay, not so good. "And how am I supposed to find that?"

"It's in your diaries."

I jumped. "You read them?"

Rust nodded. "Hey, I was very bored by myself. I found this."

I looked at a string of coordinates. "What are these?"

"Star charts. Where the the mothership is, where the emperor is. You take it out, the Imposters will never be able to destroy Earth. Never be able to go to other planets. Hidden in your words, I found out where this ship is. Since you have it, it makes sense that the ones nearest you have it too. Your friends will have the same information if you get them to write. If you do that and give them to me, I'll find the rest of what we need to know. And then, we'll go to the source. And wipe it out."

I still didn't really get this. "So, I'm going back in time, not to kick ass and attack, but to ask my friends to write in diaries?"

Rust laughed. "Yep. Oh, and to kick ass. You'll have to find the creatures that I've fought to contain. When you get back there, I'll be your best ally. I'll take what you say at face value. Your body in the past will remain where it is. You are the only one strong enough to endure the trip, which is why I can't come with you. My younger, more dapper self will be of more use."

Ah, he anticipated my question. "So, I go back. Tell everyone…"

Rust had his most disapproving face on.

"What?" I demanded.

"The Being of Time isn't one for everyone knowing how it turns out. You can't tell anyone more than me. Just trust me on this. It's too dangerous. One false move, and you might not change anything."

I filed away all the information in my head. Don't tell anyone. Get them to write in diaries. That'd be fun. Fight some new threat I have no idea about. And finally, give my info to Rust to find out where we will take on the Imposters. Fun, fun times.

CHAPTER 3

I expected a long training sequence with me finding out how to deal with the telepathic communication device I was supposed to use to contact Time. I thought Rust would pull down one of those screens and start lecturing. Instead, he said, "This is the Journeyer. Okay, hop in. I'll make the adjustments."

I sucked my lips in. "Don't I need to know how it works?"

Rust shook his head. "No way. I've waited a hundred years for this moment. I want it to disappear."

That sounded good. *Not.* "Disappear?"

"This world. Undone. Like it never existed. All the pain. All my suffering. All my loss… Except for my parents. Can't undo that."

I pondered that as I sat down in the comfortable chair. He pulled the helmet down to squash against my scalp and Mond's clear face went over mine. I closed my eyes and imagined his real face being this close. I'd see him again. I wouldn't worry about burning him now.

I was just way too old for him. I hated thoughts like that.

Wandering fluttering birds of annoyance reminded me that life was pretty bleak. I ignored it. I wanted to see Mond. I wouldn't think about how much older I was, technically.

"Why not?" I suddenly said. "Why not go back to when this started? Get rid of those Imposters before they even put one toe on this Earth. Kill Molly before her jealous head rose."

Rust pulled some strange-looking tubes up and used the suction ends to attach to the skin under my chin. "Three reasons, I'd say. One is that so many things have happened thanks to this course of events. Long streams of history. People coming together. Creating children. And more. Like Gem. No Breathers, no Gem."

That got me. If I went back too far, nothing would be the same. I recalled a similar conversation that I had with Natalie. At that time, I had said I chose this life. I did. I wouldn't risk going back in time to stop that.

"The second reason is that I'm not sure anything less than full-out war with everyone on Earth involved would be able to stop them at that time. There have been losses on both sides, but when the Imposters came to Earth, they came ready for battle. Now—or at least the time you're going back to—they have grown a bit complacent, relaxed, not ready for anything but an invasion."

I nodded. He pushed a button and a strange platform rose out of the floor with lots of gauges on it. He checked my heart. And my pulse. Plus, my Burner power stage. Not making it up. It was written right under a number that stayed high.

Before I asked what it was, I had to know the third reason. "What's the last one?"

He knew what I meant. "Moral questions, really. Do you kill before a crime is committed? Isn't it wrong to end a life when that life is technically innocent?"

I shook my head. "It already happened! We know it did."

Rust wriggled his shoulders. "Still doesn't feel right. Kind of like playing God. Crime first, then punishment."

I would have argued that time wasn't linear, so why shouldn't justice be the same when one of my readings rose. "Hey, what's happening there?" I asked.

Rust looked at the number and smiled. "It's your fluctuation. This gauge tells me how healthy you are with your Burner powers. You are good. And as the food moves through you, it keeps you at top status. And believe me, you'll need it."

Rust pushed three levers up at the same time and a hum echoed throughout the room, vibrating in my skull. My head was pressed against the back of the chair, comfortable at least, but I couldn't move.

"Okay, it's on and ready to go. Just think of it as a phone call. Talk to whatever you can find. Then ask."

"And then?" I bit out.

"Beg."

The walls melted and pulled away from me. Everything fell out until I was floating in negative space. None of my limbs worked. Swirls of color exploded in my eyes, the mysteries of the universe. The swirls became lines and were woven into tapestries. If I could just get close enough, I could read them, could tell what they were.

But I was falling, like Alice, waiting for the white rabbit to appear. Clocks exploded in my eyes. Ribbons danced into chunks of marshmallow.

Instinctively, I pulled up my ice to shield myself from the chaos, the insanity. Now, I knew why the others failed. My grip on reality was falling apart.

Pandas became chickens. Robots attacked planets. Nothing was real. Everything was real. I flew and fell. Ran and stood still. Stars slipped into my skin and made new solar systems in my hands.

I shook with all the materials hitting me and yelled, "Please. Help me!"

Hills appeared, and I landed. In the sky. The hills above me. My feet on blue sky with clouds underneath. A cat appeared. A big cat. Giant moonlike eyes and a chin that drooped.

"Time?" I asked. I had no other speech.

"I build worlds. I dictate life. The end and the beginning are the same. What is a being I control doing here? Why do you talk to me?"

"I need a favor."

The cat laughed, rolled upside down, and dug in the sky, clawing out comets and space dust. It flew through the air, hitting me in the eye. Wrapping paper made me a gift, a bow on my head. I pulled another layer of ice up. Mental ice.

There was no here. I was still in Rust's fiery building. This was all in my mind. I needed protection.

"Why would I do a favor for you?" Time asked.

"Because..." Well, I had no reason for that. I could only yell. "You ruined my time! I had very little happiness. Balance. There should be balance. I lost my parents at six. Lost friends later. Saw people die. I got Mond for only a year. And he's gone again. It's not fair!"

Wow, and I thought I was a mature seventeen-year-old! How could Time even think beyond my tantrum? I was choosing a very bad tactic.

The cat rolled in the sky, eating its own tail until it disappeared. Then it appeared again. "I don't think about lives. I think about order. The universe goes in one direction."

"Not true!" I yelped as I floated there, encased in ice. "Time isn't linear. You could put me back. Or are you so weak you can't change the course of time? What a fool I am! Of course you only answer to someone else."

I tried to figure out how to leave, to stop this communication. The cat's face became all I saw, growing bigger and bigger until there was no sky, no hills, just me in its space eyes with moons around me.

"You dare to mock me? Others have come here. They have talked to me. They have respect. They beg me with their puny lives to help. I have said no. Every time."

"Oh, whatever." I didn't want to talk to this stupid cat-slash-Time anymore. It was hopeless, as usual. I didn't want to be here. But come to think of it, I didn't want to be there either. If I couldn't get back in time, this thing was over.

"I'm sorry," I said quickly. "I just need this, or I will cease to exist."

"Speak no more. I admire bravery and, yes, rudeness. When a lesser being, so far below a higher one, doesn't bow down but still offers respect, that is the hope for the future. And I like the idea of another future. I will do this for you."

I breathed out nothing because I wasn't really there. But a cool blanket of relief cuddled into me.

"There are rules. You need to follow them, or the very fabric of time could break apart. First, you may stay for only the length of a week. Your presence is not supposed to be. Once a week runs out, you'll return to the time you're in for the same amount, and then you can go back. All of this will last for about seven times."

"Okay." I didn't want to rock the boat by asking why that was.

"The being you were will still exist inside the building in New York, so you will be out of time, technically in two places as the future goes on. If anyone finds out who you truly are, time will pull you back, and you won't be able to return to the past. Then, of course, the original time will come back, and since you in the machine will still exist, you will cease to be."

Okay, this secret was serious. I couldn't tell Mond. I thought Rust was just kidding about that. That would be hard, but not impossible.

"What about Rust? He told me I could get his help."

Time moved, or nodded, or whatever. "He exists in both times. No one else does. You are stretched across time. All beings are. As long as the body exists, the particles are connected. Anyone else who exists in both times can be told. Can be your ally."

"Anything else?"

"You are not immortal. Die, and everything changes back."

I didn't care. This was working! I had woken up to such pain—I had left so much misery! I was being given a second chance. A chance to live again with all my abilities, with my friends. With Mond.

"Can I call you Time? Or would you rather I use another name?"

I heard the breath of a sigh. A universe ending and beginning. "I have no use for a name. An appellation is a brief conceit, a differentiation between beings to recognize each other. I am one. I am unique. There is no other me and no other being contains me. I am over all. Under none. I need no names."

"Okay, Time it is then," I said.

Was there amusement in the being's mouth when it answered? "One more thing. You make your choice. When do you want to go back?"

I considered this. I hadn't had a lot of time to think when was best. But if I went back before Molly's death, would I still, I don't know, have that electricity sickness that drained me? Or would I be okay? Any earlier, and I might be tempted to change too much. Erin's parents. Me being taken away.

And the thought chilled me to the bone. I had never felt so cold like this. Not in my life. I was never cold. But…I could ruin everything. I could save myself and ruin others. Rust was right. There were too many events. I needed to stop just one.

The event that made the world like this, that had killed so many and made humans slaves.

"I need to go back, uh, please," I said. It couldn't hurt to be polite now. "To right after Redmond and the others left my machine, the Burner Augmenter. Like a few weeks. Can you send me to their location?"

Time nodded. Or, at least, the cat rolled its head on the horizon.

Everything turned upside down. Or right side up. I was on the hills now.

I blinked and returned to where Rust was.

His face fell. "Didn't it work?"

I opened my mouth—I exploded.

All my pieces went in different directions.

I became the walls. Or maybe the sky. I watched as Time moved its back and then arched. Things moved backward. Rust and I eating. Leaving the fiery building backward. Me waking up—going back to sleep.

The buildings reversed being destroyed. New York rose up around me. Traffic soared in tandem.

My pieces melted and bled until I saw the new place. The island! That's where they retreated back to. Of course. It made sense. The only peaceful place for us.

I wondered how long we had before the invasion. I dropped down onto sandy shores. A castaway of Time. The salt air tickled my nose. The sand felt almost soft against my head.

I didn't move. No one was here right now. I was by myself. Together again. My same body. Nothing about me had changed. I was still a hundred and seventeen years old, back to only a year after I left the island.

I was home.

And I had to save the world.

CHAPTER 4

I stayed on the beach, enjoying the sun. It was warm. And I wasn't cold, as usual.

It didn't take long before I was noticed. I must have been quite the sight. A time-mussed girl with long white hair in a fancy ball gown lying on the beach as if I were in a swimsuit.

The first clue I noticed was a shout. Only minutes later, I was surrounded.

It was like I had seen them yesterday. But for them, it was much different.

Mond pushed past everyone to see me, his mouth falling open as I got to my feet.

"Oni!" he yelped. Barked. Or maybe screamed. He was next to me in seconds, pulling me into a bear hug and swinging me around. I was flying.

"Amazing! You found us! You look great! Only a few months, huh? I expected longer. Your hair was only like one-tenth white. Oh!" He squeezed me to his chest, kissing my hair and forehead. Everything was right again. My fire was back.

"Okay, I don't want to interrupt," Natalie said with a large grin on her face. "But this reaction is going to get more physical in a minute, and we all want to welcome you back."

Mond wouldn't let go, but he stood by my shoulder so others could kind of give me a group hug. Natalie first. Then Nora, Cindy, and even Erin gave me a tight hug before pulling away. She was never one to be comfortable with her emotions.

"How'd you get here?" Nora asked. I saw a whole lot of Burners behind her. More and more were coming. Way down the beach, I saw Mom, Drake, and Gem all breaking into a run.

My appearance had caused a storm of emotions. I was not used to this!

"I froze the water," I said quickly. I wasn't accustomed to lying. But I had to get good at it fast. I wouldn't have this ruined. Seeing all of them together, accepting the hug from Mom and Gem when they got close enough and maneuvered around Mond, I remembered where or when I had come from. Where everybody was dead.

Minus Rust, who was across the way. Young. Looking like an Earther and not a Simrulian at all.

"Come on," I said, trying to laugh. I wanted to cry. "You didn't really think I was going anywhere, did you?"

Cindy laughed and clapped my shoulder. "Not me! She's our hero. We gotta create a song for you or something. Laoni the ice Burner..." Cindy started in a high soprano.

I put a halt to that immediately. "I need rest. Okay. I've been in..." The future. Where all of you died from a secret invasion that is coming soon.

"Yeah, we know," Mond said. I felt his emotion pouring over me. "Give her some air, people. There's a room for you. I made sure we kept one open."

It was like a parade as I walked down the sandy beaches,

under the low-hanging trees. Very soon after, we reached the edge of the farms, which looked better than ever, and not far after that was the path that led to the row of houses for Burners.

"I can't believe you're here," Mond murmured again and again. I wished very much we could have been alone for our reunion. Then again, maybe it was best not to be. I needed to focus. I only had a short time before Time would pull me back. I needed to change things as fast as possible. The diaries had to be started. All my friends had to start writing so I could give them to Rust.

Speaking of Rust, he knew nothing, and I had to enlighten him.

"Uh, thanks, Mond," I said, pulling away. "But I think Rust should look me over. I mean, I was dying before." *As were all of you*, my hidden thoughts reminded me.

Rust was by my elbow in seconds. "Happy to oblige. I thought you needed it anyway, but some people..." His eyes cast toward Natalie. "Thought you should rest first."

"You should," Natalie said. Her face was light. Happy.

"No, I think I need a checkup. Could you?" I asked Rust. "In private," I added to my adoring fans who were trailing me. They got the point. We were alone when we walked up the narrow stairs into the doctor's cabin.

I hurt Mond. I know I did. He expected a tearful and physical reunion, spending days on our own. But I couldn't give it to him. Worse, I couldn't even explain why.

Plenty of time for that, I decided. In our new future.

A million questions hit my head. Would I be in the new future? Wouldn't it continue as normal, me in the Burner Augmenter? Would they be able to bring me out? Would Mond be dead anyway because a hundred years passed before I woke up ready to get out?

My war must have shown on my face because when I

hopped up on the examination table after changing into a pale blue hospital gown, Rust immediately asked, "What is it? Are you in pain?"

"No. Rust..." I stared into his eyes. Funny, I had never seen the whites before. They were shaded with a light green. How was I going to tell him this? He might have been an alien who lost his parents and had to grow up with a war on his shoulders, but he was still tied up in the rules of our lives now.

The kindness that stared back gave me courage. I recognized those eyes as the man who had lived a hundred years to save our world, who had fought for the first forty of his life to protect and defend people who weren't his.

"You were pushed out of New York?" I started.

Rust scratched his head and grabbed an ear light thingy to look inside. "Yeah. But I thought you'd want to ask Redmond about that. I'm just an outsider to this whole thing."

"Tell me what happened." I was warming up to giving him a major blow. There was something different to the eyes that looked me over. His weren't filled to overflowing with pain. I would start that pain now.

"Well, as you might know, Redmond got the scent on him when Paul breathed it in from underneath. Paul knew where we were. He was bringing a whole lot of Breathers with him to finish the battle. We caught wind of that and had to run. Natalie made the decision to leave you there, but Redmond... He kicked up a storm with his anger. He even wanted to stay with you. But Natalie reminded him that wherever he was, Paul would follow."

Rust peered inside my ears. He knocked my knees to check my reflexes. He scanned me like he had once before, using a red beam from his wrist. No sign of the future machine. He must have invented it later. His eyes widened as he saw how well I was doing. "You are doing way better than I thought you would," he admitted.

"What is that?" I asked, stalling.

"Oh? My scanner? An old piece of tech from my own planet. It learns about the person, tells me about sicknesses or diseases. It's still functioning. One day, it might not anymore."

I knew when. That's why he didn't use it in the future. Like everything else, the tech had died out from use and new stuff had to take its place.

"You came back to the island." I couldn't get off track.

"Oh, well, yes. I volunteered to be the doctor. A few Burners got wounded on the way back. Big battle. Boring, really, but we held our own. Paul escaped, as usual."

I clarified. "I mean, you all decided to come to the island."

Rust lifted my arms and tapped from fingers to shoulder. "It was the safest. Paul can survive. It's what he's good at. And there are more than we thought. Breathers. Riders. All secreted away. Waiting for a chance to come out of the woodwork. Natalie thought it best to stay where we were all safe. I have to admit, Burners can't live in the real world."

I was quiet. "So, what have you been doing?"

"Fixing boo-boos." He grinned.

I shook my head. "All of you."

"Living. That's all we can do. Redmond's been the worst. Hiding out, not leaving his room."

I smiled. I could imagine why. He was thinking. Trying to come up with all the machines he'd invent someday. "Rust, there's an invasion force out there. In the stars, waiting to attack. They will, but I'm not sure when."

Rust's head snapped back. "Pardon me?"

"They win. All of our friends die. I am not the Laoni you

think I am. Let's just say if you checked her Burner status, it wouldn't be that number. It'd be low. Really low. Even now she… I float in a Burner Augmenter."

Rust laughed. "That's funny."

"You sent me back. You lived for a hundred years to right what went wrong. I'm here now to do it. You know the Imposters. They didn't just infiltrate Earth. They're waiting. They'll attack."

Rust snapped his next instrument closed, whatever it was, and hopped up onto a table not far from mine. "You're serious? I don't get it. Time travel isn't real."

"Time is a creature that controls our future and present and past. It sent me here to do what I can. Rust…I can't tell anyone else. You're the only person left alive."

Rust tugged on his scratchy red hair, mulling it over. "Okay. Then what do we do?"

Wow, Rust was right. He did take things easily. "I need your help. Your parents left coded messages inside the Burners' minds. They say where the ship is, but not much else. The rest will come from…"

Rust caught on. "It's all in their brains. We need to encourage them to write in diaries."

I gave a grin. "And that will be almost impossible. Erin doesn't want records left behind. Natalie looks at me like I'm crazy. Mond will be easy, but…"

Rust pursed his lips. "I can help with a lot of them. They think I'm a miracle worker. If I tell Natalie that it's for the health of the Burners, she will do it. I can convince her and the other Burners who like me for some reason. But…" He stared at me with a small smile.

"Erin," I finished.

"Yes. But if you're right and the codes are in there, I need a lot of words. Personal and emotional. That's how my parents would hide them. The main part of the brain would be easily found. They'd speak about it. It'd slip out in conversation. Trust me, I would have noticed. If you want codes, they have to confess deep secrets and pain."

"Well, that should be easy enough," I said. Then we both laughed.

It felt good to have Rust on my side. Someone who could help me. As much as I loved Mond, he wasn't in the future. He was dead.

I needed to prevent that from happening.

Rust and I separated. I got myself some new clothes, and we both took on the task of getting our friends to write in their diaries. I had to hand it to Rust. He made it like a new religion. That writing diaries was the way to be cool.

I only had to convince Erin.

"Nope!" she said as she dug in the soil. She was replacing the sand with some enriched soil so she could plant seeds. It was time to sow on the little island. The farms stretched out far behind the row of buildings, stopping only when the sand of the beach started. Ever since Erin's parents' death, this was the only time I saw peace on her face. I wondered how long it had been for her. For me, it had been recent and a hundred or more years ago.

"But nobody will get it here," I argued. "And you need to emote. Do you even share your deepest pain with Cindy?"

"Sometimes," she said, kneeling in the dirt and rubbing her forehead to leave a smear. "But some things I don't want anyone to know, okay? You want to give me that bag of seeds?"

I knelt down next to her, pulling the bag with me. "Where's everyone else? Don't they want to plant?"

Erin gave me a not-so-nice grin. "They know I like to be alone."

"A perfect time to write!"

She snarled at me and pushed seeds into the ground,

rubbing the soil over them and then heading to the front where the irrigation system started. The whole system squeaked as she turned it on. Wet soil filled my nostrils. Each row filled with water, sparkling in the sun. "I won't. It's stupid. Anyone could find it and use it against me. Don't you realize that if I searched your room or Mond's, I could find out what you really thought of me? Way too dangerous."

I bit my lip and tried to help plant. It only earned me a glare from Erin, so I let my hands fall. I reveled in the sun on my face. I had changed back into the special clothes that helped with my ice, a brown skirt that flared at my knees with a strappy green shirt. My hair was tied up. But I could have lost all my clothing and still felt the sun on my face. Whatever my body did before, the out-of-control ice it made, was gone, thanks to my many years in the augmenter. I wondered if it would do that to my friends.

Or if I'd ever find out.

I cleared my throat. "Still, you haven't been able to talk about…" I couldn't continue, not with the glare she gave me. "Have you mourned? Have your siblings?"

She didn't answer. I didn't expect her to.

I suddenly got an idea. "Okay, if you're too scared, then I won't say anymore."

Erin's jaw dropped. She turned off the water, letting it go down its many paths to feed the soil. "I'm not afraid, just cautious."

"You think you're not scary enough. That anyone who wants to read your words wouldn't care about your wrath. I understand. Though, I thought you weren't a coward. My mistake."

Erin stood up. She looked dangerous right now. Ready to burn my head off if she could. "I am not afraid. You want me to write? I'll join the new craze and write. Then will you leave me alone? It won't help my feelings. I won't be any different."

I hid my triumph. All I needed was for her to write. Unfortunately, I'd then do exactly what she was afraid of and steal it and read her secret thoughts and feelings.

And hopefully, I'd find the real secret. How to save us all.

CHAPTER 5

ERIN

Hi. I'm here. What in the hell am I supposed to write in here? Should I introduce myself? Okay, I'm Erin Barclay, age seventeen. Fire Burner. I'm done now.

***

It's been a day. Laoni let me have it for writing only a few sentences. I hate writing! Anyone could see this. Nope. Not going to do it.

***

Hi, Diary. You are my friend. Nonsense. Laoni told me to talk to this thing like it was my best friend. Best friends aren't words on paper! They're people. Flesh and blood. People you die for. This is so stupid.

~~*

Laoni called me a coward again. I am not scared of writing in this stupid diary thing. You want feelings? I'm not doing well, okay? There. I wrote it down. I didn't think it'd be so easy.

~~*

I paused for a second because I just read what I wrote. I'm not doing well. I can't even describe what admitting that did to me.

Like a weight has lifted from my chest. Whoosh! Maybe Laoni was onto something. No way.

But maybe. I'm not a coward, so I'm going to write about what happened today. Laoni's appearance yesterday was incredible. I can't really admit it to anyone else, but my heart felt like it could beat again. I thought our hero was dead. Our hero? Great, I sound like Cindy.

Cindy. I can't go two seconds without thinking about her. Wondering what she's doing while I'm writing this. Wondering if she'd want to see this. I can't believe I can be so obsessed with her and still remain me.

So, feelings time. But I want to scream every time her wonderfully shiny eyes turn to Laoni and she goes, "Wow." I used to be the only one who wowed her. When we were together in the facility, waiting to die, we knew Laoni would come back. She wasn't dead. She was going to save all of us.

I was the one who suggested training our powers without those restraining clothes to be ready for the war when Laoni came back. Every single day, Cindy was impressed with me. I miss those days!

There, I admitted it.

Back then, I could imagine going back to my family. Cindy and I were in our world, the tops. I wasn't ready for the deaths that came.

Mom and Dad.

Okay, this stuff is hard. Writing my emotions down in a diary is bringing them back. I miss Mom and Dad! I saw my childhood home collapse on Mom. Saw Dad shot down. It haunts my mind. At night, I wake up screaming. Cindy holds me until I stop.

I, of course, put on a brave face and say I was dreaming about Breathers, but it's Dad's shocked face. It's Mom's hand lifeless under the rubble.

I don't know how to live without them!

What's worse, Butch and Carolyn are so different. They stare out at the ocean most days, as if waiting for an order. I remember Butch. My older brother. He never stopped smiling. He made dad jokes so often I always teased him he should have children. He hasn't cracked one joke since his time in the Flyers' place.

Carolyn had been so young, but she had been so curious. Always exploring. She watches the ocean without moving for hours on end. The doctor, Rust Smythe, tells me the nanoments should be destroyed by now, ripped away by their natural healing abilities. But these aren't the brother and sister I remember, or the ones who greeted me when I went home.

They're different.

Oh, yeah, and speaking of which... Laoni, if you're reading this, I'll never forgive you! Ever. I don't want anyone reading my thoughts. Maybe I should destroy...

No. I'm not a coward! I'm not. I'll kill anyone who dares read my diaries. Journals. Yes, that sounds better. Diary is a twelve-year-old pouring thoughts out. I am making a journal.

Back to what I was writing. My siblings aren't the only ones who are different. Redmond sees it too. Laoni is strange. She was supposed to be in that Burner Augmenter for years before she could be even halfway back. But she is back. With a vengeance. I'm concerned. Her hair is fully white. She keeps talking to Doctor Smythe.

She stares at all of us like we're strangers.

And she is so damned insistent that we all write in journals like she does. She's never been so much a...uh, totalitarian before. In fact, she hated being a leader. I could see it on her face. A reluctant hero. But now, she won't let up.

If she's not hounding me about writing in this thing, she's hounding others. All of us on the island. She wants a library of journals. So strange.

Plus, she and Redmond were attached at the hip before this. She'd never leave him alone. But though she's been with him, every waking hour is either chivvying us into writing like it's a life-or-death scenario or in whispered conversation with Doctor Smythe.

Everyone's different.

Except Cindy. Great. I'm smiling as I write about her. What do I feel about her? She's my best friend. My heart. My life. Now, this is easy. I am totally in love with her. She won't hear it. I can't say it. It'd make me look weak. I can't look weak in front of her. She'd look to Laoni more and more.

I have a tenuous enough grasp on my girlfriend. I can't let her slip away.

Oh, crap. Did I really just write that much in something I thought was stupid? Did I really just admit so much? Crap, crap, crap. I am going to throw it away.

~*~

It's been a day. Laoni is watching me. Or she has her ice watching me.

I am not kidding! She has placed ice tracers around, and they watch. Really! Okay, maybe I'm a bit paranoid. But I saw a mound of ice right when I was about to burn this thing and it doused the flame every time I tried.

Truth is, I'm glad. There's something comforting about reading what I've written even with a fear that it will get in the wrong hands.

I'm concerned about Laoni. She's strange. Watching us. Training. Ignoring her boyfriend and running around the island checking things. Each day, she grows more antsy. It's weird. She still acts like we're at war.

Are we at war? Is that what this is? I have to admit here and now, I had gotten used to an easy life. When Laoni saved us all and filled me in on what she had been doing since she ran away, I realized how good we all had it.

When we were in the facility, I acted like we were at war, that we'd save the world. But when we ran, I saw how truly evil our enemies were.

When I was ripped out of my bed, I knew my parents would suffer. I spent the rest of my life trying to get back to them. Now, I realize I was playing games while Laoni was out there actually winning the war. I felt so damned sure that I could make a difference. I was always telling everyone exactly what to think. But Laoni was right to be in denial. Because I'd love some of that about now.

Can't get there. Can't hide from the fact that who I was trying to get back to died defending me of all people, a Burner. Someone who can burn the very air around. But I just stood there, helpless, getting grabbed by a Flyer and whisked away. Useless, that's what I am.

Just useless old Erin who plays war games. I remember Laoni getting mad at me, way back when. "Why do you have to be so down all the time?" she'd ask.

I had just thought she was being incredibly naïve. But no. I was the naïve one. To think we could win. To think I could ever succeed in getting back what I lost.

I should have been the one to die at sixteen, not Belinda. She did the real work. Made ways for us to escape. Only Laoni found them. She never gave up. Never stopped.

I had sat around and waited to be saved.

Useless. Pathetic. Just a wannabe hero.

~~*

It's night. I had to grab this. We're leaving on a mission tomorrow. Cindy's staying on the island. Thank you, whatever. I won't have to worry about her. Keep her safe. There's another facility we're going after. Laoni asked Natalie to look into it.

It's a weird one. I don't even know how Laoni knew about it. There are different Breathers there.

I don't know how different, and I don't care. I'll burn anything.

I have to ask though. Will this ever end? I never wanted a war. I wanted to be safe. To get out. To get revenge for Belinda and then settle down. The island... When Laoni mentioned it, I was so happy. Wow, that is hard for me to say. I haven't been happy in years.

But, anyway, I thought...peace. An end to the violence. I thought we'd get my family, and we'd all live happily ever after. But no. Laoni went out to fight again. When I saw her leaving, I followed.

Stupid me. I can't let it go. Like I'm some kind of hero. I'm not. I don't even want to fight. I just know what Cindy would say if I said to let the world hang. She'd turn her shiny eyes away from me.

Don't get me wrong. I can pour my whole heart out here. I don't want people to suffer. I would hate to think that when I was in the facility that someone was out there, and they refused to help me to save their own peace. That's why I continue on.

I'm just so afraid. Maybe I am a coward. I've lost so many people already. I don't want to lose Cindy. What would she think about me and my not-so-noble thoughts? What would she have said when Natalie asked if I wanted to go with Laoni and Redmond to liberate more Burners and I said that I wanted to stay here?

She'd like Laoni better than me. She's already so close. I'd lose her.

So, I'll go into battle. I'll die if I have to. I don't want to lose the shine that is in Cindy's eyes when she looks at me. I don't want to lose her love.

Because what else is there to love about me? I get angry easily. I failed at saving my own parents. I didn't protect Belinda when I knew something bad was going to happen.

I hate myself. Why would anyone love me?

Damnit. I'm crying now. I hate tears. All they do is make my eyes puffy and my nose full of snot. I won't write anymore. I can't even believe I can write all this out. It makes me see myself in a new light. And it's not very flattering.

Maybe I can change. I have to think about this. Ponder. Laoni once hated me for being so much of a realist. A pessimist, she called it. But I don't know what else to be.

Could I be like Laoni? Or am I doomed to be useless?

You know what? I think I'll write again. To figure all this out. I just hope no one ever reads this.

I'd kill them.

CHAPTER 6

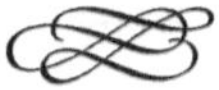

The submarine hums quietly through the water as I write in my diary. I hope there's more in my own brain that Rust can find. Natalie has something in this sub that tells her if other ships are in the area. I'm holding hands with Redmond. It seems nice now. I'm against his back, blocking the diary from his view, but I feel at peace. Right here, right now, that horrible future is gone, and I can be with him. Soon enough, it'll be time for battle.

Ever since Rust, in the future, told me about the new Breathers, I have been on edge. Like or hate the original—mostly hate them—I know how to handle them. But vampires and werewolves? So not my expertise!

I had asked Natalie to check on weirder things out there, not exactly Breathers. For her to not look at the usual stuff. She gave me a weird look and left on the first submarine. When she came back, I wasn't at all surprised to find out she had discovered a new facility of Burners.

Top secret stuff. Guarded by…animals.

We were headed toward the deep woods. Trees surrounded the facility. I could tell that my friends wondered how I knew. Natalie had asked me a few times to talk to her, to tell her exactly how I got out of the Burner Augmenter, how I got to the island without the submarine, and why I hadn't just contacted them.

She had left messages, it turned out, at the New York building I was still in, the present me.

I lied. I keep lying. It's even hard to be with Mond now. His eyes are searching me, wondering why I didn't want the tearful and hug-filled reunion with him he wanted with me.

I don't think any of them trust me now. Maybe Cindy. But she can't stop. I'm pretty sure Erin's going to kill me one day. Joking! But maybe not.

How can I help it? If I tell any of them, I'll kill all of them.

The truth is a pathway, but lies are an obstacle. I'm pushing all my friends away. I have to build up brambles around the truth. I can't fail. I won't. I wonder what the end result will be. With peace in my mind, I can't help thinking about the end.

Erin's staring at me with narrow eyes. I can feel it. But I can't tell her.

Diary, I feel like their enemy. But I'm not! I'm going to save all of them.

CHAPTER 7

The submarine slipped into hidden waters. The plan was to hike a long way, deeper into the woods. We all were given food and water, just in case. We didn't need to get lost and die of hunger and thirst, of all things. I had never been inside woods as deep and dark as this. The shadowy trees roared above me. Leaves almost obliterated the starry sky.

We went two by two, shoulder to shoulder, following the path that Natalie was making. There was a natural one, but the facility was to the north. And sometimes, she had to hack through. Natalie was a funny sort. She had claimed to be completely devoid of power, minus the ice form she could bring up from time to time, but even now, she hacked through leaves and branches with an ice machete made from the lingering droplets of water on the trees.

I wasn't surprised to see that Mond was my buddy, but there was a gulf between us, and it was growing wider. He knew I was lying to him, he just didn't know why. My heart would have broken in two if it hadn't already, far in the future when there was no legacy of him. No child. No future. He would die so young.

Erin and Bobby were behind us. And Natalie and a fire Burner, Wally, were at the front.

Natalie kept us at a slow jog. Quick but not too fast.

It wasn't long before I felt the danger.

Movement shuffled through the trees, surrounding us. Natalie picked up the pace, but I got ready for battle.

They knew we were here. And I was the only one who knew what was around us.

I broke my pace with Mond and rushed up toward Natalie, slipping between her and Wally, who, with respect, fell back.

"Natalie…"

She grimaced at me, hacking a big chunk of leaves and stems out of her way. "I know."

"Bait," I hissed out, and she got it in a second.

"Okay!" she shouted loud enough for whatever was following us to hear as well. "Laoni and Erin, stay here. Redmond, Wally, Bobby, and I will move forward. Guard our rear."

Redmond didn't say anything, but I could feel in his tense form that he didn't like the idea of leaving us behind. But Redmond had learned. He and the others slipped away into the trees. Erin stared at me.

"What's going on?" she whispered.

"We're bait," I said under my breath.

"Why us?" But she tensed, starting to roll out fire at her feet, looking for a natural burn.

"Why not?" I asked.

The trees groaned around us. Lots more than I thought dropped from branches above us and slunk out of the shadows.

I was not surprised to see Paul. "Are you everywhere I don't want to be?" I demanded.

Paul gave me a grin. He looked worse for the wear, to be honest. All Breathers were attractive, and with his shaggy brown hair and cleft chin, Paul could easily sell clothes for a living, but he now sported a thick scar from his temple to his chin, and he was much more ragged.

"You look good," I mocked.

He shrugged. "Mortality catching up."

That startled me. Breathers… How long did they live?

"But I'll survive. I'm surprised to see you, I have to admit. You were dead, weren't you?"

"I came back. What's up with you?"

He gestured to his friends, who were silent but easing up on us. Sniffing the air. Smelling *us*.

"You haven't seen these, have you? Freaks me out. I have no clue why the Riders wanted to bring these creatures of hell to life. I think they're fans of supernatural books or something."

Okay, so the Imposters read our books. Who knew?

"Don't be rude," a new voice added. This Breather was taller than Paul. Pale skin. Fangs in… Oh. "Aren't you going to introduce us?"

"Hi, I'm Laoni," I said brightly. "The one contemplating your swift demises is Erin."

He gave a full smile, showing his fangs. "The sight of you makes me glad my makers put in the ability to drain blood. Why are you here? It's obvious you are Fire and Ice Burners. I can smell it."

I glanced to my left and right. There were more vampires than just the one talking, and at their sides were two or three people—uh, Breathers—who were in a crouched position. Tufts of fur reached out from behind their ears and fell down to their backs. They only wore clothes on their front, and I could see their broad backs covered in fur. What in the hell had the Imposters been doing?

"We've come to join your facility," I said. "I wanted to see how they lived."

"She's lying, Lev!" Paul announced.

"Oh, gee, really?" he asked, giving him a withering stare. "You've come to steal the kids back, haven't you?"

I gave a broad smile and gestured. Snow started dropping on them all, covering the area in white. I was good. "Ding, ding, ding! You win a prize. Cold, yet?"

Lev snarled. Hmm, yes, much more demonic than any Breather I had ever met. The evil showed on their faces, unlike the others. I would have never fallen for this guy's charm.

"I've got the Ice Burner," Lev said.

"By all means," Paul agreed and stayed back.

Lev spread his hands and jumped at me—

Only to be met by a punch from Redmond. He wouldn't let anyone near me. Lev and Redmond fell to the floor in a violent scuffle. Fire leaped up around them, and I sure hoped the ability to catch our scent was taken away from these new Breathers.

Howls erupted around me as Bobby and Erin stood back-to-back, ripping tree branches down with fire.

But I knew. There was no way the Imposters had given these Breathers all the powers. If they could have, there would be an ultimate weapon. They had been hidden away, never sent into battle.

These Breathers were failures. That's why they were kept secret.

"Use your full force," I yelled to my group as a werewolf pulled me down. "They can't absorb it."

Then all hell broke loose. All the Fire Burners with us could burn. And they did. Without hesitating, their flames ripped through the night, burning our enemy.

Yes, I would have liked to talk to the idiot Imposters who thought these creatures up. By even mythical info, fire was the enemy of the supernatural.

They ran if they could. We regrouped and stared at each other. Paul was long gone, as usual.

"That was horrible," Natalie said with a deep frown.

"It was incredible!" Erin laughed. "I could finally just burn them. No absorption. No chance of them coming after us later."

"It was unfair and horrible." Natalie wasn't happy. "They stood no chance against us."

"They were evil," Erin responded.

I remembered what Rust had said. "That wasn't their fault." I had been caught up in the battle before. With the nasty Breathers like Farrell and Digory, I had rarely felt guilty for ending their lives. Or hurting them.

But these creatures brought it home for me. They had been made in facilities and forced into a mental attitude they didn't choose. Now they were either dead or burned beyond recognition.

"Are you seriously defending our enemy?" Mond asked. The expression on his face wasn't pleasant.

"No," Natalie answered for me. "We're here to save people. They were trying to stop us. I just don't feel as if this was the greatest victory. Let's move, people. Let's save the ones we came here for."

She turned around and we headed north again.

But I saw the look in Redmond's eyes. He hadn't been talking to Natalie. He was talking to me. He wanted to know what side I was on.

I couldn't tell him how I knew about these creatures being just victims in a game started by Molly. I had to keep that a secret. Because the info came from the future. Where I wasn't supposed to have come from.

We charged through the woods into a huge clearing. In the middle was a big building, two stories high, with many windows. A large grassy field met the foundation, but stymieing entry was a tall metal fence with many sharp edges. Just like the facility I grew up in, it had a whole lot of security to keep Burners in.

We melted it in seconds. A group of Fire Burners can do that.

The walls followed afterward. The smell of melting metal and building material mixed in the air. We charged inside and came across a whole lot of tired Burner children, looking at us with sleep in their eyes. Innocent to what was going to happen. Funnily, I saw no place where the machine would go, the draining one that would kill them at sixteen.

"You, get them," Natalie ordered Redmond to two little black-haired girls who were staring at us with big eyes.

"Don't worry," Redmond said. "We're just going on a little trip. Would you like to see a cool island?"

"Where's Lev?" one asked. My heart went out to him. I would have asked that same question, except about Farrell, way back when. My parents had betrayed me and Farrell had taken the role of father. Before he had switched to murderer.

"We're just moving," I said quickly. I had had enough of feeling like a kidnapper. "Lev wants us all to meet him on the island. You can go for a swim there and play on sandy beaches."

The boy's eyes lit up, but he looked at all of us with a whole lot of suspicion. We didn't have time for this. I was running low on time. Three days had passed. I had four to change something. Somehow, I didn't think saving these kids made even a blip on the radar of the future.

I looked into my powers. I had so much. I didn't even know how. That Burner Augmenter had given me almost unlimited powers.

I snapped my fingers. Every child there, whether still in bed, over Redmond's shoulder, or walking toward us, became ice. Little statues of humanity. And I knew I could restore them.

Too bad my friends didn't.

"What the hell did you just do?" Redmond demanded.

"Easier cargo. We can stack them in the submarine. There will be no struggle. In case you couldn't tell, they are happy here! We are taking them away. Through the dark and scary woods, into a cramped submarine, to an island with no contact from the outside world. We can't coddle them the whole way. Now they're cargo, not children."

Redmond gasped. Bobby stared at me. Wally didn't look happy either. Only Erin and Natalie looked relieved.

"Can you bring them back?" Natalie asked briskly.

"Yes, I can."

Redmond was staring at me, peeling away the layers of my mind with just his will. But he didn't recognize me. I almost didn't myself. But I wouldn't have my mission ruined by a waste of time.

I had thought rescuing the kids was the best way to go. That something here would have helped. But everything in me told me I had just wasted two days with nothing to show for it. This didn't feel like a rescue mission. We had destroyed a weaponless foe, grabbed kids who didn't want us, and escaped like criminals. This wasn't good, no way, no how. Hopefully the diaries did something. I had to wait to see. But I couldn't just let the last days of this week fall away.

I couldn't waste it by traveling slowly through these

woods, comforting children who didn't want to leave their home, and fighting off attackers. We had to get in, get out.

I made a humongous ice litter where we did as I said and, uh, stacked the frozen children one by one and dragged the litter through the path we had made.

I was at the front with Natalie this time, and Redmond stayed behind me.

I was making him hate me. I hated myself. I couldn't even do anything but what I thought would work. If making him hate me was the price I paid for saving his life, then I'd do it. I had to.

Still, I couldn't stop my tears from falling as I pulled my ice rope next to Natalie.

"You're right," she muttered. "We had to do it this way."

Maybe. But tell that to my aching heart, who wanted to run back to the end of the line and promise Mond I wasn't as much of a monster as he thought of me right now. But I had no choice. I was alone in this.

As we reached the submarine, we put the kids in place and shoved off. I stayed in my little sub room, ignoring everyone and even myself. I thought through what I had learned on this journey.

A few things troubled me. One, Paul. He did look bad. How long did Breathers live? And would he finally be put out of my hair soon? I sure hoped so. He was an irritant who kept showing up at the worst times. And he had Redmond's scent.

Two, if these kids were Fire Burners, or even Ice, how could they submit so utterly to my ice? You'd think one would burn their way out. I could have. Erin could have. It didn't make much sense. Were these Burners as much a failure as the Breathers that guarded them?

Then the final missing piece of the puzzle. Even if I could

save them all, would I be able to live at the end of this? Or would I lose all of them anyway?

Everything swirled inside my head, making a storm of snow and ice as I cried. I couldn't stop thinking about those poor kids, treated like frozen fish sticks and taken where they didn't want to be. I missed Mond. I missed his arms around me. I missed my world. Why did everything have to be so hard?

CHAPTER 8

NATALIE

The children have been unfrozen successfully. Thawed out? I do have to admit that Laoni is more powerful than I am. Of course, I have repressed my powers for years and years, as has Nora. We haven't liked our ice since Molly...

Could we have had the abilities of Laoni? If we really tried hard enough? I have to get back to training, I guess. Or eating properly. Stupid Rust. He's aggravating. What's worse is that he's right. You know, I have never written in a diary like this. Laoni is sure insistent. When she looks at me, I see desperation in her eyes. I have to listen.

But she wants me to write about my emotions. Feelings, nothing more than feelings. Yeah, that's me. Only Nora knows how much pain I've got inside. But she's even more tightly wound than I am. At least I still use the powers we now feel cursed with.

I remember when we were young. The pranks we pulled. Freezing over the fountain in that fancy hotel. The people had been staring in awe. Touching it. Walking on it.

Then we let it unfreeze. The people got in trouble for swimming in it. Nora and I laughed so hard that day.

Molly hadn't. I still remember her glowering at us. Now, I don't dare use my powers like that. I lied to Laoni. I'll admit it here. I told her we lose our powers as we age. That wasn't true. I just haven't known a lot of Burners live to our ages.

Nora and I have repressed our powers for years. They may be helpful now, but at one time, they ruined our lives. Destroyed our parents. Molly was the one who killed them, but it was because of our ice. How much Mom and Dad loved the stuff we used to do. The little ice plays we put on.

I pulled out an ice machete in the woods on the way to fight vampires and werewolves. Did I really just write that? Okay, manipulate the elements around me? Great! Riders who have the ultimate technology and turn out to be aliens? Fine. Breathers who hunt us down? I can accept that. But vampires who suck your blood? Werewolves that are animals mixed with humans? Somehow things just got so much weirder.

I feel tension on our island. Laoni is different. She and Redmond were such young lovers, hanging on every word the other would say. Now, Redmond watches her with narrow eyes, growing more and more distrustful of her.

I'd talk to him if I thought I could give any wisdom. People change when suffering happens. Laoni has suffered, maybe more than any of us. I don't know.

I told him, "Laoni did die, you know." And she did. We would have lost her if it hadn't been for Redmond bringing her back. But she's still here. My surrogate daughter. I feel a motherly connection with her. Maybe because I helped her grow or showed her what a mature Ice Burner could be.

She's still the same noble spirit I first met. But now she has the weight of the world on her shoulders.

But Redmond swears she's lying to all of us. I don't buy it. Yes, there is the fact that she said that the Breathers aren't at fault for their evil. I don't know how much that's true. And yes, she has been spending an awful lot of time with the newest member of this group of ours, the alien.

But Rust isn't bad. He's growing on me. I go for check-ups more than I would care to admit anywhere but here. Yes, I can admit it here. I am supposed to be talking about my feelings. Rust is interesting. His freckles move when he's speaking. I catch myself staring at them. When he puts his hands on me...

No, I won't confess even my secret thoughts here. Rust is an annoying alien. That's it.

Back to what's happening. Hopefully, lusting after my alien doctor isn't needed for whatever it is Laoni needs this for in the first place.

We returned to the island, unstacked the frozen children and lined them up. There was quite the commotion when they thawed out. Crying, screaming. I tried to tell them it was okay, but they wouldn't listen. They acted as if we were kidnappers. I've never had much patience with explaining things. Redmond tried to tell all of them, and he and Cindy played games until the children calmed down. There are twelve in total, ranging from seven years of age to twelve. Nowhere near sixteen. Good. But not so good. They didn't believe there was any danger.

We knew there was.

Vampires? Come on! What is the logical conclusion with vampires and people? That's right. Those children were going to be meals. I'm glad we got them out.

Laoni concerns me, though. She won't let me in on what she's worried about. And she is worried. Damned worried. Terrified. All she does is walk the island. When she talks to anyone but Rust, she just tells us to write in our diaries.

And how did she even know about this strange facility? As far as I could tell, there's never been any info about anything except Breathers. But Laoni swore there were things we didn't know about, creatures that didn't fit into the usual Breather modus operandi. I was skeptical. She looked so...sure. How did she know?

I didn't even know there were more out there. Me! Some protector-slash-guardian. But when I checked with 0142, who has been very helpful since losing her programming—though there are times when she just stares at nothing, like she's waiting for an order—she checked the internal computer in her mind for any information of feral Breathers and found that place.

It was a failed experiment. There was only one place like it in the world. But Laoni knew it existed somewhere.

What exactly happened to her in that Burner Augmenter?

It's a wild night tonight. Far across from my cabin, we've got crying children who want to go home. We've got Laoni walking aimlessly around the island. She'll probably reluctantly go to her cabin and fall into bed sometime. I'm not keeping a watch on her. Not when we've got Redmond following her, looking absolutely miserable. I can't go around wondering if I have enemies in my backyard. I need to believe that there are two sides: One, good, Burners; two, bad, Breathers.

But then again, Laoni's stepfather is a Breather. And there have been a few Burners who had crossed over to the evil side.

No! I can't not trust Laoni. She's our rock that holds this whole blasted thing together. Hadn't I given up? Hadn't I let people die for years just to save my own skin—oh, and I guess the ones on the island. It's just so hard. I try to ignore it. It just keeps coming, doesn't it? The hits.

My life has changed thanks to strange aliens bringing war to my home. Rusty's parents. He, too, has had a life. I swore I'd never care for anyone as deeply as him, my first love. The Burner who lived through the machine taking... It's horrible. I haven't thought about him in so long. Laoni's state had brought it all back. I miss him...but I forgot him. Life has been a battle where reminiscing or longing is as stupid as taking on Breathers.

But now? Fine. If I am to be honest anywhere, I'll do it here. Laoni wants it. The reason behind it is strange, but I trust her. She needs me to emote. So, here I go. I want Rust. I like his hands on me way too much. Sometimes during his examinations, I have these incredibly inappropriate thoughts. I think he feels it too. But his parents died for my kind—Earthers, that is. And I live with ice in my veins, thanks to his parents. In a strange way, we both have taken things away from each other. Our kinds, anyway. Can we get past that? Do I want to?

It's all so new. He is so aggravating. Am I really wondering how to tell him I'd like some alone time with him? Do I dare love again when I watched my first love die in front of me? Because Rust can die. Our lives aren't meant to last. It's only by the wildest chance that either of us is alive.

Okay, Nora is weighing in. She thinks I should go for it. I told her to stay out of my business and my head. Should I go for it, though? This is so incredibly aggravating. War though it may be, this armistice is bringing thoughts into my head that I don't know how to handle.

Lucky for both of us, though, there's no time for romance. Just war. It's still out there. I can feel it. And with how Laoni is acting, the battle isn't done. No, it's getting warmed up.

Back to my main problem. Redmond. I'm scared of him. Not because he'll hurt me, but because I'm afraid of what's going on inside his head. It was bad enough when we had to leave Laoni.

But this is worse. He is starting to...think of her as an enemy. I need to have a talking to with him about that. There are no enemies on this island.

I have to believe that. Erin's brother and sister concern me more than Laoni. They are quiet and shy, never really joining in, and they stare out to sea. Sometimes, I swear I hear whirring come from them. But it's not possible.

See! I'm growing as paranoid and distrustful as Redmond.

My years on the run, helping Burners get to the island, making the Bed and Breakfast I loved until it was destroyed. I don't want to be a gigantic cynic waiting for the next bad thing to happen. I have to admit we've done really well for ourselves.

We have our island refuge. We have our friends. Life seems just a bit brighter with Rust. I mean, having a doctor to help with illness and injuries has helped relieve the stress of having anyone gravely wounded.

Laoni survived a death sentence. We destroyed a lot of breeding grounds. We're not hiding out here. We're just avoiding a Breather that has Redmond's scent. But we could easily deal with him.

When I was alone, communicating only with Nora, and running my B and B, I felt like life was pointless. That all we did was wait for death. I knew that Burners were reaching sixteen across the country and being murdered, and I couldn't save them.

But we have. We've stopped these new children from being eaten, of blood or flesh. We've liberated more than a dozen young Burners.

We're growing an army. Soon with training, all these kids could take back our world. Send those stinking Riders back to theirs.

Yes, I'm optimistic. I have to be.

I love these people way too much to imagine anything bad happening to them.

And yet...I worry. All the time. I don't dare feel happy for too long. I don't deserve it. Not after what happened. Not when it was basically my and Nora's fault that Molly became that way. Always showing off. Never allowing her in.

I hate her. But she's dead. I...never...mourned her. She was our villain. But she was our sister. Nora...what do we do?

Ah, yes, I got a response. Nora tells me we do what we've always done. Live for protecting. Vow to get rid of what Molly did. Maybe then our own guilt will be absolved. Nora's writing in her diary too. We do a lot of things like that in unison without telling the other.

It's strange. Nora and I are the only Burners with a psychic connection. It has served us well. Even far apart, we are together always.

I'm going to bed now. There's always tomorrow. Maybe I won't feel so utterly ashamed when I look at the kids in the morning.

Goodnight, Nora. Don't let the bedbugs bite. She hates it when I say that to her before I go to bed, and I do it just to, heh heh, bug her. Maybe I'm still only twelve years old. I don't care.

Diary done.

CHAPTER 9

I stayed with the children overnight. I didn't want to see Redmond. I had to make sure I kept away from Rust too. I could tell the others were starting to get suspicious. It made sense. What would I have in common with an alien doctor who no one, except me, was sure whose side he was on?

The kids latched onto me. Funny, considering I was the one who turned them into frozen statues. They blamed it all on Natalie. She was easy to blame, one of the only adults present. Most of them didn't want to get into the bunks we had for them. They curled up next to me and held my hands.

"I miss Lev," Bee said. She was a little girl, small for her age, with a pointed chin and broad forehead.

"You don't understand," I said slowly. "They were going to hurt you. We were saving you."

"No one was going to hurt us," Bee scoffed.

The little boy I convinced first, Gino, nodded. "They don't come back," he noted. He was curled up at my knee. I sat cross-legged in front of the group. The wooden beams under me were uncomfortable, but the kids didn't seem to mind.

"They graduate," Bee insisted.

I cringed. "No, they don't."

"Uh-huh!" Bee insisted. "My sister turned last week."

I cocked my head at her. "Did you see her again?"

Bee surprised me and nodded. "Yeah. She had fangs. She was chosen to be a vampire. I'm going to be a werewolf. I asked Lev if it was okay."

I blanched. So, that was the thing at the facility. No draining. No energy taken. They were turned.

"But what about your ice? Your fire?" I fingered the material of the clothing Bee still wore. She refused to let us give her new stuff. It wasn't the material that had contained my ice way back when.

Bee laughed. "Ice and fire? I don't know what you're talking about."

I stared at her. "You don't have abilities?"

This was a big mistake. I didn't even know how big of one.

Gino tugged on my jeans. "We don't have parents. Is that an ability?"

I looked around at all of them. "None of you have parents?"

"We're foster kids. Some of us have parents, but they don't care," Gino said. "Others lost parents. Lev brought us to his home so we could be remade."

I suddenly understood our mistake. There had been no Burners there, only failed Breathers. And they got kids who weren't wanted to continue on. This wasn't our world. This wasn't our history. All these kids had a different story.

I clasped my hands together as the kids fell asleep.

I was wrong. Whatever happened in the future, these Breathers weren't the same as the ones I knew. Farrell and his relentless pursuit of me. Digory and his mean streak. Lev didn't sound the same. He wasn't kidnapping children from their homes or buying them. He was saving them. At least, that's what these kids thought.

The area was a bit morally gray. Were they hurting these kids? Bee didn't seem to think her sister was a monster now.

I closed my eyes and drifted off, wondering what to do. I had changed nothing about the future except make every one of my friends write in diaries. They seemed to be getting into it. Only Erin truly hated it. Everyone else did it for me, and, of course, whatever I wanted, I got. I was still their hero.

For all except Redmond. I could feel his glares.

I wished I could just go and find him. Give him a few dozen kisses to prove I wasn't evil. But I couldn't. The lies between us hurt my heart. Redmond could feel it. And I could feel his pain.

This whole thing was a mess. Four days in, and I had no clue how to stop the future insanity that would hit our world.

It didn't get any better for the next three. All I could do was ask questions. This island was a dead end. I had to get off it to find out anything.

How was the question. There were no plans to go anywhere, and everyone was settling down.

Not the new kids, however. They seemed to think our Burner status was weird. Bee screamed out loud when Redmond showed her a fire horse. They didn't want to be here. And they hated everyone but me.

I wanted to scream as my time ran out. The seven days ended, and I could feel Time arching its back.

Things moved forward again, but I could only see a blur of light and colors. My skin was wrapped in a cocoon, and I tripped back to Rust's home base. Old Rust looked up. He was reading a book.

"So, you weren't successful," he noted.

I looked at the outside rubble. No, I hadn't been successful. "Nope. You've got me for a week. Let's figure out what happened. Did you read the diaries yet?"

"Oh, of course. We figured out... Wow. I have two memories. It turns out I'm somewhat outside of time with you. But I only read yours before. New memories are shifting and aligning now that you're back."

"Rust. What went wrong? What do I have to do?"

Rust sighed. "Let's talk."

CHAPTER 10

*J*had to admit that we were both down about the first attempt. Rust hadn't said anything, and I wouldn't. But we had both thought I would solve this whole thing the first time going back.

But little had changed. The diaries helped a lot. There were a whole lot of schematics for the secret alien warship hovering out there somewhere. But there was a lot missing, like how to get to said spaceship and, more importantly, how to bring it down.

The week I had to wait to go back was the longest of my life. Every second was a minute, the minutes were hours, and, well, you get the idea.

All I did was wander around Mond's building, reveling in his heat but despairing. I knew he wasn't here where I was. Even in the past, he wasn't with me. Maybe our relationship was over.

That wounded my heart. But what else could I do? This way, I'd save him.

"Okay, one more time," I said with my chin placed glumly in my hands. "What happened in this history?"

We were in the living room again, basically trapped in this place thanks to the constant flyovers the Imposters had. Besides, I had nowhere to go. What was the use of looking over everything that had gone into ruin?

"The same thing I've already said." Rust smoothed his wrinkles with his index finger. Resistant, they popped right back into place as he let his hand settle. He had cards in his other hand. To pass the time, I suggested *War*. Rust seemed to like it even though it never ended. "The Imposters had a secret warship, but also had Breathers infiltrating the entire world. With one signal, they all attacked at the same time and killed Burners and any humans who fought back.

"After a long resistance, we succumbed to the sheer number of them."

I laid down an ace and took Rust's cards. As he opened his mouth to object—he really didn't get the concept of losing—I distracted him. "But what about the island? Why didn't you all just stay there?"

He blinked, widening his eyes. "Oh, after it was compromised, we couldn't stay there."

I dropped my cards. That was the first I had heard about that. "They found us? But I thought…"

"That it was our best hideout? It was." He let his cards drop too. Who wanted to play *War* when a real one had happened and destroyed everything? So far, I was doing a terrific job of stopping it. The loss of our paradise, our home, our hideout, carved a path down my heart.

"But that rescue of the kids from the supernatural facility…"

I gaped at him. This was all new. I had changed something. Of course! None of my friends had known about the secret failed Breathers until I had told them. "That rescue was a mistake?"

"More than." Rust dragged his fingers through his green hair. It fell with heavier thuds than I'd expected. "After about a month, the kids figured out a way to send a secret message to their friends. The Breathers came and attacked. They wanted their kids back. It was a horrible escapade. Cindy died in the attack."

My heart froze. I knew they had all died in this future, but Erin had lost so much. To imagine another loss for her. Somehow, I didn't think she'd recover from it. Erin was my friend. So was Cindy. Her loss hurt on so many levels.

"What is it?" Rust asked.

"You'd think I get used to the fact that everybody died. But this is so much worse. Because it's my fault. I told Natalie to look around and find that place. I drew them to the island." I picked up my cards again. Then I threw them across the room, flat, square, icy missiles that embedded in the wall and didn't melt.

"Well, go back and fix it." Rust seemed to think that was so damned easy.

"Time is not interested in giving me multiple chances. It's done. A one-time thing, but maybe…"

Okay, time to jot down a mental list. When I went back, the first order of business was to return the kids before they drew their friends to our hideout. We couldn't do anything if we had to be on the run. And, of course, the second was to end this war before it started. I didn't want to return a failure again.

Too bad I had no idea how to do that.

Out of nowhere, an angry beeping sound filled my ears. Red flashed through the area. "What is that?" I asked.

Rust surprised me and rolled his eyes. "Long story, but there is one Breather who survived these many years. One who is a pain in my hair." Rust jumped up and ran through the area. I had no choice but to follow him. A Breather survived? Which one...

I groaned out loud as I figured it out.

"Paul," I said as I got near Rust's shoulder and he opened the door to the outside.

"You got it. He has remained an annoyance. He stays true to his programming even though it's been many years since he was last called upon."

I scanned right and left. "But that makes zero sense!"

Rust nodded. "All the other Breathers live fifty years max. Their systems run down and they die in a pool of their own juices."

"Lovely thought," I grimaced.

"Paul, however, learned a few tricks to stay alive. Remember the Neo Breather you killed?"

I jumped at the moniker I gave a horrible monster that consisted of sucked-in Breathers making an overall whole. "Yes."

"Paul figured out that right before the birthing stage, he could take the goop they secreted and use it to, uh, absorb their bodies, giving him more strength and a longer life. Needless to say, the higher-ups didn't approve. He became a rogue agent, continuing only based on the evil inside."

I shook my head. Like I should feel sympathy for that yucky Breather. "Where is he now?"

"He attacks this place every so often. He thinks I am the last vestige of a war. He's smarter than I give him credit for. He thinks if he ends my life, he ends the resistance."

"How wrong he is," I said. The horror I had lived with for the last few months transformed into pure hatred. Paul was a great target. "Can I freeze him?"

Rust suddenly aimed and fired. I saw movement around one of the dunes of rubble. "Same rules apply. You hit him, he gets your scent."

I punched my own hand. Without asking, I took Rust's gun and charged out the front, dodging the piles of rubble best I could. Detritus from the ages spread out in dusty remnants all around. It exploded in my nostrils. Dust, dirt, rubble. Dead ends.

Flashes of movement led me on. It felt great to run, to stalk a Breather for a change. I wanted more action, and I could do nothing in the past for fear of ruining the future. But this was the future.

"Come out, come out, and play!" I said in a singsong voice.

Paul actually listened. I was surprised, to say the least. He looked better but worse. Like the monster in Frankenstein, made up of purely beautiful parts but on the whole so wildly disconcerting, he was ugly. His hair was velvety brown, shining with a starlike glow. His eyes were...yuck, like looking into a Neo-Breather's eyes. Paul's were gone. Six or seven pupils were separated by white with a mashed color set. But that was the only way to tell he was augmented to be like the Neo Breather had been.

"Laoni!" he said. "They told me you were dead. I missed you!"

I gaped and then hissed. I hated these stinking Breathers! "Say cheese!" I snapped and fired a yellow beam of pure energy. Somehow, I wasn't surprised to see him do a backflip to dodge it.

"No, really!" Paul said as he landed. "It's been so long. Who knew my greatest adversary would survive too! It makes me happy. So many of my friends have died."

Something I had never felt for a Breather was tapping me on the heart. What Rust had said... Molly had filled the Breathers with her evil. They had no choice but to attack. Paul had no choice...

I fired the gun again.

Paul dodged it again.

Rust came from behind and tackled him, holding his arms behind his back as best he could. The old guy didn't have much left, but he used all his strength.

"Now!" Rust grunted. "Shoot him. Get him out of here."

I aimed, cocked the trigger, and stopped. Paul bucked Rust off him and ran away. A normal trait of Paul.

"What were you thinking?" Rust demanded, getting up and dusting rubble off his reddish vest.

"He didn't have a choice. All his friends are dead." I couldn't put it into words. I didn't even understand it myself. I had wanted to kill him. To take all my anger and pain and put it into a destructive beam that would end that miserable Breather's life. But I couldn't.

Somehow, someway, Paul never had a choice. None of them did. Farrell, Digory, Paul. The ones who kidnapped all of us, programmed and murdered us, living half as much time as a human would, all to be weapons.

It just felt incredibly wrong to be the one to end the life of someone so interested in staying alive.

Rust gave a wry grin. "You're becoming touched by all the tragedy. To see someone worth saving who is born evil."

I smiled back. It felt forced, but I didn't want to get rusty. Soon, I'd smile for real. I just knew it.

"So, back to the diaries," I said, and we both walked back inside. Paul wouldn't come back today. He was a survivor, and he knew I could have killed him. "Are you sure there is so much information missing? All of them wrote. Do I need someone else?"

Rust shook his head as the outer doorway closed. "No. My parents wouldn't spread out the information. They would have known there could be trouble if it were separated. It's in the past. In your friend's diaries. Either they aren't emoting as much as you think, or someone isn't doing their part."

I glared at him as he sat down again, the cards and our game of *War* completely forgotten. We needed a board game or something. Maybe Life. I had always loved it when I played it with Bobby way back when in the facility. "You've read them. I haven't. Are they emoting?"

He pursed his lips. "Yes and no. I mean, I get Natalie is. She admitted..." He looked away, sadness in every breath. "Nothing. But she's being honest. And Erin is too. Most of them are. Just one might not be. Every diary entry of his feels like a lie. You'll have to deal with that when you go back. Oh, and you'll start all over again. The diaries stopped when you disappeared. You'll have to explain your absence and get them back on track."

Great! That sounded fun. I already had stubborn-as-mules resistance. Now I had to make them continue. After I disappeared. "Whose are lies? I can knuckle down on them more than anyone else."

He gave me an almost coquettish look. "Your boyfriend. Redmond tells lies. You haven't checked up on him, have you?"

"Of course not!" I barked. "I can't tell him the truth. That's all I want to do. I can't deal with him if I have to lie mostly. He's giving me such..."

I tried to hold back my tears. I was becoming way too weepy now that I could actually cry. I didn't want to. I had a mission. I had to be strong.

"He doesn't trust you. Not too surprising, is it?" Rust looked at the worn coffee table in front of us and walked slowly to a cabinet that held tools. He took some sandpaper out and started rubbing the corner. "You and he used to be closer than anyone I could ever name. If you're pulling away, he'll feel it. It makes your job tougher, but I don't see any other way. Just hold on. The truth will set us free. One day."

Would it? One day... Could I tell the truth after this whole thing was averted? I had to talk to Time some more. I hadn't gotten a lot of answers. I stood up and walked off. It served Rust well he didn't ask where I was going. But I needed to ask Time for more information and maybe another favor.

CHAPTER 11

A chicken was wearing a suit as it pecked at miles and miles of eyes. Yep, I was back in the mental realm where I could find Time. I wasn't flying, but I felt no control over where I went. Caught in a current. Unable to stop it.

No! That wasn't me. I could stop it. I wasn't trapped by this realm.

Focusing more on my internal mind and not on the insanity around me, I pulled up ice again. In this place, I had infinite control. A motorcycle popped up under me, gleaming of ice, sending off smoky vapors as I climbed on board.

Setting my jaw, I drove.

It wasn't like on a real road. There was nothing under me except chaos. But I had a direction toward Time.

Funny, now I was bringing myself to Time and not the other way around.

My nonexistent tires skipped against the equally nonexistent road, skidding to a stop in front of…

Not a cat this time. Now, it was a gigantic stone sculpture, feminine in appearance. Her eyes were empty as she sat with her hands on her knees. Almost unreachable. Bigger than anything I had ever seen.

"Time!" I said, pretending I was standing. So, I was. "I have a few questions."

"I have told you more than any human. I have given you more than any mortal has ever dared to ask for."

I snorted. Hey, there was nothing left to lose anymore. Time tolerated me. That was the best I could get. "I know, and I truly appreciate it. But I just need to know. What happens at the end of all this? Do I stay? Return to my time?"

Time shifted. Stone creaked as the giant woman stood up, sinking down like quicksand pulled at her. Slowly, her orb-less eyes stared at me. "You want to know if you succeed? But what if you fail?"

I stared back. "Not an option."

"How you deal with me is unusual. Very few people have ever tried at all, but when they do, they're almost turned out of their own minds. How do you have the strength to look me in the eyes so boldly?"

I had no clue. I wasn't aware that I was doing anything irreverent. All I could answer was, "Time, I've lost everything. I was supposed to die. Me. Not anyone else. But as I woke up to this horrible world, I can't believe I'm in it. It's wrong. I have accepted a lot of changes in my life. Being abandoned by my parents. Hunted and tortured by Breathers and Riders. I know that I was born with a target on my back. You know what, fine!

"But to lose him. To lose all of them. I don't deserve this. I deserve the right to be happy! So, yeah, if I have to look you straight in the eyes and demand stuff, then I'll do it. I don't *want* to fix this. I *need* to. I have no other choice. If not, then I will die. Just tell me…how much can I hope to stay there? Will you let me stay in the past after I change the future?"

Time reached out a big stony brown hand and lifted me up to peer into her eyes. "You are a thorn in that time. It is a wound. A minor one, but you can't stay."

My heart sank. I had expected as much.

"This is why you can only go back for a week and then remain in this time for another one. Every trip back rips a hole; the longer you stay, the more it bleeds. Do what you must to take your world back. But you will not reap the benefits."

I rubbed my imaginary eyes. I wouldn't cry fake tears here. I'd wait until this was all over. If I couldn't remain in the past, I'd be in the Burner Augmenter. When would I get out? Would I even be aware of how much I lost? Worse, would they ever get me out if they thought I was already?

So much of the future was unknown. I couldn't dwell on it, though. "Time, I... Could you just let me tell one person the truth? Redmond hates me. He doesn't think I'm a friend. I don't want him to..."

I couldn't finish my statement. Suddenly I was spiraling back the way I came, thrust out by Time. The force was so intense I couldn't fight.

But I got the hint.

No. No one could know except Rust.

I came aware back in the chair. I rubbed my eyes. Clearly, I had been crying real tears. My cheeks were soggy.

I wandered back out to the main area.

Rust was there on the floor like he had fallen.

"Rust!" I yelled and rushed forward to help him up. When he looked at me, my mouth fell open. His eyes were red from crying, and his cheeks were rather wet too. "What happened?"

"Nothing. You weren't supposed to see this. I thought you'd be in the machine for a while."

I pulled his thin arm to push him onto the couch. I got up

next to him and held my face to his shoulder. "Why are you crying?"

Rust sighed. "I always cry. When the weight of the world comes upon me, when I lose all hope. Every day. I lived when they all died. The Burners. Natalie... I see her face. She died in my arms, you know. I saw her light flicker out. That has remained with me. Stuck inside my mind. I cry to get it out. Never helps."

I felt more comfortable with Rust than ever before. Grief can draw people together; when two people have suffered the same, they speak to each other without words. "You seem so happy most of the time. I had no idea Natalie's death would hurt you the most."

He stared at me, and suddenly I got it. The years I had been gone had brought the good doctor and my surrogate mom closer together. Very close. He cleared his throat and answered me as he rubbed the remaining tears from his eyes. "Hers hurt me like I lost my arm. Her absence in my life is living without the sun." Rust let his head fall. "I live on a mission. I will do anything to save her. But there are times..."

I tried not to cry myself. "Like when I came back a failure."

"No." Rust turned to me. His strange eyes peered into mine. "You didn't fail. You delayed. You will succeed. I know it."

His head bent down to reach mine, and our foreheads touched. Rust was becoming more to me than just an alien. He was my friend. He was almost family. We had been bonded by so much shared grief. He was my hope. I was his.

I couldn't fight against his hopes. "So, will you marry her? I want to make sure your intentions are honorable."

Rust pulled back and gave me an incredulous look. "What, now?"

"Natalie. You're right. I am going to succeed. And when I do, you'll be stuck with her. No one-night stand type of stuff, got me?"

That earned a chuckle. And just like that, Rust was back to the silly guy he had always been. "Dammit! I didn't think about that. I had the great excuse of her dying to make sure it wasn't anything serious. But now, I'll just have to put a ring on her finger, won't I?"

We laughed together. For that one moment, everything was good. It would work out. There was no reason to doubt.

But as we both went to bed, doubt came back. I went to my room and fell onto the square mattress. There were so many things that could go wrong. It already had! First, the rescue of the children. I had to correct that.

In addition, what would happen to me? I had lived to this future. Would I do it again, just to a happier one? Would I return only to find Redmond's grandkids telling me stories about their grandpa who had a fling with an Ice Burner who betrayed him?

I couldn't sleep. And as Time's caress reached inside me again and tossed me back in time, I shut everything down. I had a mission. I didn't care what the consequences would be as long as I saved him.

As long as I saved them all.

CHAPTER 12

I was lucky. Nobody was around again as I fell onto the beach. Maybe I should have asked Time to put me gently into my bed. Then again, I wasn't sure who would be in it. Or if I could even garner more favors from the being who threw me out so utterly.

I tiptoed around the island. It was dark, the water around it only known by the sounds of waves gently reaching the shore. A light wind blew, the sound of which made a tiny howl through the leaves. The smell was the same. I breathed it in, remembering my first time here. Me and Mond together. Now, we were so far apart. But I could still feel his arms around me, us both smelling the salt of the ocean around us.

But the past wasn't important. At least not the stuff I couldn't change. I was here for a reason, not to reminisce. I wasn't heading for my bed. I was heading for the kids. I hoped they were still here.

But nothing had changed. The cabin they were in was still and quiet. Through the windows, I saw all of them asleep in their beds. As I crept closer to their windows, I heard the sounds of nightmares. They hated it here. The kids taken from the supernatural facility were still all snuggled together.

"You're back? You want to tell me where you went?"

I jumped high into the sky. How had I missed Redmond? I turned around a faced him. I had no lies ready. I had to think fast.

He was leaning against a tree, a flame on his finger sparking in and out of life. My heart leaped and sank. He looked gorgeous. He had freshly cut his hair to his shoulders. Still a little shaggy, but I had been used to him with long hair, and it did something to my stomach. His face was ruggedly handsome, illuminated by the flame and then darkening again. He wore shorts that showed off his knees and a loose button-up shirt.

I wanted to leap into his arms and give him a few kisses. But it was clear he had no desire for me.

"Um, hey. Didn't you see me? I was around. I just…" I racked my brain. I should have come up with an for my weeklong absence before I arrived. "I was practicing underwater with my ice. I sank down almost to the bottom and stayed there, just to see if I could. In fact, that's where I just came from. I am exhausted."

I stared into his eyes to see how he was taking it. I guess my explanation was so impossible, it was plausible. It was the kind of thing I'd do in peacetime.

"Oh. Why didn't you tell me? I've…missed you. Before. And now that you're here, I still miss you. Why is that?"

I couldn't believe that he believed me. Okay, the kids had to wait. I couldn't let Redmond feel bad anymore. Not tonight. I rushed forward, wrapped my arms around his chest, and placed my cheek against his bare skin. So warm. "I'm sorry. I've missed you too."

I guess the feeling in my voice convinced him. He tilted

my chin up and hungrily searched my eyes, looking for something. I looked away. I was scared he'd see my lies. But he closed the gap between us and pulled my lips to his.

This I remembered!

No burning. Nothing hurting either of us. Perfectly compatible. He brought his lips to my chin and kissed me on my neck.

"Laoni," he whispered. "What aren't you telling me?'

Just like that, the mood was ruined. I couldn't tell him.

I pulled away and put one hand on his chest. "Nothing," I said innocently. "I just wanted to hone my powers."

His face fell to anger again. "You are already too powerful. And come to think of it, how? You got out of the Burner Augmenter so early. Now you are…"

I turned and walked off. He stayed against the tree.

I couldn't say anything more. How could I tell him anything without jeopardizing my very position in time? It was a harsh reminder. I couldn't stay and enjoy the sweet caresses of my boyfriend. I had a job to do. Besides, he wasn't *mine*.

My boyfriend died at forty. The one who was supposed to be with this Redmond was the one inside the Augmenter.

And I had to ensure her world was there when she woke up.

I walked around until I could see Redmond from far away. He looked shell-shocked. I had given him nothing.

As he walked away, presumably to go to bed, I turned my mind on. It was time to get these kids back home before my mistake became real.

I froze everything in sight as I walked into the kids' cabin. All at once, they were back to being kidsicles.

I had thought about this while I was in the future. I couldn't drive the submarine. I'd barely learned to drive a car recently. But what I could do was use my powers. I had a whole lot at my disposal.

So, an hour later, I had stacked all the kids inside the submarine and was submerging. I could do that, at least.

It was a good thing that it was night when I returned. I couldn't have hidden the fact that I was dragging a litter of frozen children and putting them in the sub. Anyone could have seen me and demanded to know what was going on. I was too busy trying to ensure I missed none of the kids who would betray this island one day.

Finally, we were being propelled through the water by my very own icy hand, pushing us forward. I was getting better at geography. Or maybe I had no choice. I had to remember where their home was. These kids were going home.

I had to do this.

I just hoped I'd get a good reception when I came back. I started thinking of an explanation because this would not go down well if I couldn't give a good reason for returning the kids.

My life had sure gotten complicated.

I wasn't the most intelligent person in the world. I thought I was indefatigable. Super-powered and could do anything with ice. Maybe I could. But that didn't give me infinite energy. When I finally returned to where the kids came from, I yawned in the darkness as I dragged the litter under the dense foliage above me. I made icy ropes that fit over my shoulders and crossed my chest in an X and trudged on, pulling my frozen cargo behind me.

I sure hoped the Breathers here would accept my explanation before attacking me. I had to admit it didn't look good. But I had no other choice. At least the children were off the island, unaware of our hideout, which meant they couldn't compromise it. Back in the future, that had to have changed…or would have when I got back.

I didn't know why, but this physical labor brought a pensive mood. I was…depressed. I had been all go-go-go for so long, I hadn't had a chance to sit back and think. But I missed the old days. First, the ones with Mond in our little world of running and trying to find our new home. Then the ones where we were together to save the world. I missed my mom, who I had barely known. I was angry at myself that I couldn't handle all this better.

Mostly, I was terrified I was going to ruin everything. I already almost had.

I could hear every noise. Someone was following me. Or maybe it was just an animal. I had been chased for as long as I can remember. I couldn't function other than on autopilot, which meant I had shut down all my emotions. Funny how depression doesn't shut down.

The forest trees watched, full of themselves. They had friends. They were at peace. Here, they weren't in danger.

Maybe it was the long trek with so much on my back. Maybe it was the fact that I missed Mond so utterly. But I hated the trees. I envied them.

Then the shuffling started, like I had expected. I let my cargo stop. I held my hands up quickly and yelled, "I'm here for peace. They're all okay. I've come to return them safely."

Lev emerged from the shadows, his fangs prominent over his lower lip. I wasn't at all surprised to see Paul, though I was a bit confused. I mean, he had his trace on Redmond, not me. Maybe he just hung out here. Maybe they were his friends.

"How did this come to be?" Lev asked.

Paul stared at me. "Yeah, why would you bring them back?"

I surprised myself. "I'm not your enemy. I wanted these children to come home."

There was another shuffling sound in the brush, but nobody appeared. Only Lev and two others, werewolves by the look of them, were present. I ignored the noise. It was probably the same animal who was "following" me before.

Lev gave a huge grin, showing his fangs and other white teeth. "That is incredibly decent of you. But you did take them in the first place."

This I had an explanation for. If Lev were truly interested in the safety of his charges, then he'd listen to me. "I wanted them to have a better life. But they told me they had one. You see, in the facility I grew up in, we were all killed at sixteen."

Paul nodded. I saw a shadow across his eyes. "She's telling the truth. You Shadow Breathers don't know this, but Burners have immense energy in their skin. The higher-ups are using them to power amazing technology."

And probably their spaceship, I thought to myself. It hit me then that the spaceship was perhaps the end result of a few of the Burners who died. They powered the invasion. Like a lot of epiphanies I've had, though, I kept it to myself.

"Then..." Lev spoke slowly, methodically. I swear, if I didn't know he had been created, I would have thought he was a two-hundred-year-old vampire. "You were concerned that was what we were doing."

I wouldn't tell him why I was really returning the kids. I'd let him think I was being altruistic. The truth was, I'd kill all these kids if it meant a better future. I was becoming stone. I couldn't help it.

"I was until Bee told me who she was, an unwanted child."

Lev grimaced. "All of them were. We wouldn't take any

child who was wanted, loved, and protected. These were abused, neglected, ignored..."

I raised my hands. "Well, they're here now. I'm going to unfreeze them, but I'd bet they'd like to be home. So...?"

Lev got the point. "I would be honored if you would enter our facility and stay the night. No harm will come to you."

That was good, though I didn't really care. I wasn't afraid for my own safety. I was afraid for my future. If anyone tried to hurt me, I'd freeze their hearts.

Lev turned and motioned with a wiggle of his index finger that we should all follow. Paul matched my stride while the others went ahead. I watched Lev's back as I started pulling again. To my surprise, Paul lifted the ice rope off my shoulders and helped pull it.

"You look exhausted. It's strange that none of your friends came with you."

"Long story." I glanced at him. He hadn't added Neo Breathers to his arsenal yet. He still looked nice, even though he was, you know, a Breather. And not like Drake. Drake had goodness shining in his eyes. He truly loved my sister and mother. But I saw the dark evil deep within Paul's eyes. He wanted to attack me. It was just his survival instinct that held it at bay.

He held one of the ice ropes attached to the litter and glanced at it, like he was considering getting my scent by absorbing it inside.

"You do and I'll kill you," I said.

He shot me a look and pursed his lips. He knew I meant it. I was safe, at least for now.

"Comes in handy, doesn't it?" I asked.

Paul gave me a curious look. His eyebrows knitted together. "What?"

"Your sense of self-preservation. You don't have to do even a quarter of what I've seen Breathers do."

He scowled and looked away. "Are you trying to figure me out now? How sweet."

"I already have." I picked up the pace. Lev was fast, his long legs propelling him faster than I thought possible. The extra help took a lot of the burden off me. I could keep up. "You don't want this life. You do everything you can to build up your own survival. That's your defense mechanism, so you don't have to be guilty of anything truly evil."

Paul sighed. "You are psychic, too? I thought Burners only controlled elements."

I laughed, then I bit it back. No matter how pathetic his life was, I couldn't be laughing with a Breather. "No. I'm not psychic. I just… Well, you've been very annoying, but I've watched you. You talk big. You even believe it. It's your programming. But you run, like, all the time, just before real evil starts. You have to have a reason. You've run even before any danger to yourself. But you have to keep going.

"It's in your blood. Even now, you're trying to figure out a way to destroy me."

Paul blanched but nodded. I saw his eyes rake my face, full of anger and hostility, but he sighed and looked away. "I don't want these thoughts! I've never wanted to hurt anyone. But I have. So, I try to think of a way to keep my dirty hands from worsening. Survival."

He grimaced. "The thoughts I was born with don't mind me wanting to live. I have become obsessed with it. Like this stinking life is so great. You know I'll die at fifty? Not long now."

I knew that wouldn't happen. "You'll survive, if that means anything."

Paul cocked his head. He was so confused by me. I could

see why. One minute I had been ready to kill him, the next, I was reassuring him. If anyone saw us talking like this, they'd think we were old friends.

"I haven't been nice," he warned me. "I watched over the facility after Farrell didn't come back. Your friends…hate me."

I would too. But it had grown so much more complicated.

"You hate you too," I said. It was all so ridiculous. Creatures born evil right from the start, no choice. I hadn't realized how bad it could be. I had hated Farrell so utterly, but he had been almost like two people. The father that brought us all toys, who laughed as I chased him down the hall, telling him about our spy escapades. But I remembered his face as he tried to kill me. The switch turning on.

And even with Molly's death, the switch was still on. Yet… As the ground turned from dirt and leaves into gravel, I thought Paul was different from Farrell and Digory. The same evil, but different.

Molly's evil wanted more than death for any Burner who resisted. She had wanted torture. The Riders… Yeah, they were evil on their own. But the Breathers had a program. It was still running, even with the thoughts gone.

If it had only been that, I would have thought it just kept going. But I had never considered that, maybe, a new person was making the program. Like when the Flyers attacked when we liberated them. Molly had been in direct communication with them.

Maybe that thing the Journeyer had been copying, it was still in use. Someone was sending the evil.

Another epiphany! If they could, so could I! I could free Paul of his struggle and give us…

"Holy chicken dumplings," I whispered.

Paul looked toward me as Lev stopped up ahead.

"Paul, I want to help you, but you'll have to help me. Later, can you come talk to me? Just remember that I'll kill you if you attack me. I mean it."

Paul nodded. "I'll be at your door."

We couldn't talk anymore for now. We had reached the main entrance. The Shadow Breathers had been busy. I realized all the walls were repaired, and the defensive fence —meant to keep bad people out—was back in working order. The main doors opened, and I took the kids to an open area.

"This is where we take new arrivals so they don't get too scared and can be together until they're ready for a room. The kids will recognize this place." Lev nodded and gestured to my litter. "Free them. If they have been harmed…"

I knew what he'd do. He wouldn't like my blood, though. At any rate, there was no reason to worry. I brushed my hands together and the kids thawed instantly. Still asleep. I clapped my hands to wake them.

"Come on, Bee. You're home."

"She's back!" a new voice yelled, and I knew it was her sister. Dark black hair that fell to her waist. Tiny fangs that would grow. A slender form. Healthy and well, just…you know, a vampire.

The children's faces were incredible to see as they realized where they were. Hugs were thrown around, and the whole place became alive. I heard their laughs, saw their smiles. This was home. Just like the facility had been once for me. But this was different.

It was truly home, not a lie.

Once the commotion ended, Lev turned to me and gave me a warm and welcoming smile. I kind of wished he'd stop doing that. A snarl and a smile showed the same number of teeth—pointed and made for drawing blood.

"We welcome you tonight. You will be shown every

possible hospitality. I will personally show you to your room. You look, forgive the term, drained."

I held back a smile. He wasn't wrong. That drag through the forest had been exhausting.

I followed him down long corridors. "How is it you don't have the same problem with an evil mind?" I asked.

He gave me a confused look. "I do not understand."

"Your friend, Paul, is controlled by evil. Or didn't you know?"

He paused and opened a door to a nice, square, white room with a bed and a sink, homey and comfortable with knitted blankets and animal pillows. Cinnamon apple perfumed the room. Pictures of bunnies and kittens saturated the walls. "Forgive this. We usually have children coming, and our adult rooms are full."

I rolled my eyes. I heard his hidden meaning. He was afraid I'd stalk and kill him in the middle of the night if I was too close, so he wanted me far away. I thought I'd be the one to worry about that.

"And as for your question, Paul has never shown us or the children any evil. Maybe he's different with Burners. We don't get out much. This is our home, and the Riders have no use for us."

I nodded. This was indeed a different world than what I was used to. It didn't need destroying or saving. Now that I had solved the future problem of losing our island, I didn't need to have anything more to do with them.

Lev brought my hand up and kissed the back of it. "I truly appreciate you saving our children. Others may have birthed them, but they are our future. Please understand."

I nodded. I actually did understand. Too bad none of them had a future. Not according to future Rust.

Lev let the door close behind him, and I hopped up to

make sure it wasn't locked. It wasn't. I was free to leave whenever I wanted.

I fell back against the bed and tried to calm my thoughts. I had one hope today. It burned strong in my head. When Paul came, I'd put my plan into action.

As I waited, I smiled. Maybe I finally figured out something that would help!

CHAPTER 13

REDMOND

Hey,

It's Redmond here. I'm currently sitting in the elbow of a tree watching the sky. What has happened is too big for me to process. Usually, I'd lie in this diary. I don't like telling the truth. Something about Laoni felt wrong, and I didn't want to admit that. Not here.

But now I have no choice. I don't have anyone else to talk to. I get why Laoni has so many diaries. I almost wish I had woken up Bobby or Erin and asked them to come with me. When I saw Laoni icing those kids and dragging them from their cabin, I couldn't think. Only one word went through my mind.

Traitor. She was betraying all of us.

But still, there could have been an explanation. Maybe she was taking them to their real homes. I mean, they weren't Burners. They didn't belong on our island. They hated all of us. But when she took the submarine back to where we found them in the first place, I was, to say the least, baffled.

But the worst thing happened tonight. She said, and I quote, "I am not your enemy."

Excuse me? What? Laoni is the Breathers' enemy. Has been.

Always. She hates them more than Erin does, and that is a feat. For her to tell the very Breather with my scent that she isn't his enemy...

Something in me snapped. I turned around and fled.

Then I realized how stupid I was being. I had to watch Laoni, find out how much more she'd betray us. I followed her again. There she was, laughing and chatting with Paul as they dragged the kids back to the vampires and werewolves who would destroy them one day.

Where in the hell did Laoni go? The hero I know? She's gone nuts or bad. And where did she disappear to for a week? I don't believe she was under the water practicing.

I love her more than anyone I can think of. I have to give her the benefit of the doubt. But it's so hard. She looks like she's either being controlled by the Breathers or is... I can't even write it. But I will. She's their ally now. A friend. A new Breather made of a Burner.

No. That can't happen. If Burners can team up with the enemy who will destroy them...

I am almost going insane here. I want to burn, but I can't. I need answers. Laoni is staying with the Breathers, living with them! Like the old days, but this time she's seen their evil. How can she?

The sun is coming up. I think she'll leave soon.

I hope so. Because as soon as my fire tracer sends the message that she's leaving that building, I'm going to run toward the submarine and hide again.

I don't know what to do. When we left Laoni in the New York place, I wanted to end my own life. I felt like I was abandoning her. During the months on the island without her, I didn't feel human. I felt like the same animal I had been when I hid out, afraid of my own fire.

But I had to survive. I couldn't allow Laoni to wake up and come find us, only to see that I was gone. I wouldn't do that to her.

You know, I had fantasies about her. Not in that way! But she'd appear from the water like Aphrodite riding a shell. Okay, maybe a little in that way. She'd rush into my arms and we'd be together again. Even with the crazy stuff in the real world, our island home could have been our paradise. I thought this time she'd want to stay, not go help people.

But I would have been happy if she had returned and left to help Burners. Because that's Laoni.

Now, though, she's back. She appeared like I thought she would. Though, I first saw her on the beach and not on a giant shell.

But she ran away from me at every chance she got. It was like she was breaking up with me again, but this time it was because she was sick of me. It sure seemed so.

But then a weeklong disappearance. Coming back to kiss me but then abandoning me again. And now this? She's changed. She might not want me anymore! But I'm starting to wonder if she wants any of us. If she even wants the good side anymore.

I have to keep an eye on her. Something is very wrong. When I look in her eyes, all I see is devastation. No emotion. No love. Just Laoni shutting down.

Okay. My fire tracer has sent a message. Two people are moving.

Yes, two.

Paul. Laoni. Two best friends. Or more...

Ugh! No freaking way. I can't imagine them...together. No. I'd kill him. I'd do it with the sharpest knife, one piece at a time.

Gotta go. I have to either trail someone or kill someone. Maybe both.

CHAPTER 14

aul and I walked together through the forest. It was a much pleasanter place when it was morning. The sun seeped through the trees like liquid, and the air was crisp and fresh. The scurrying around was from animals, loving the morning as much as I did.

My new traveling companion gave me pause. Sure, I knew he wasn't responsible for many of his actions. But he was still going to do them. I may have scared him enough that I'd kill him if he dared move a toe toward me wrong, but how much could I rely on that?

"Mornings are the best," Paul emoted.

I nodded. I didn't want to be his best friend now. He wasn't to be trusted. I had asked him last night about the item I needed. But he refused to tell me where it was. He insisted on taking me to it.

"Look, you can stay here and enjoy it all you want if you just tell me where the, what did you call it, Cerebrander is. You don't have to come with me. It's already pretty uncomfortable being around a guy who wants to rip my skin off my body without being stuck on a small submarine with him."

Paul swung his hands as he walked. He looked so incredibly ordinary, not like the monsters that had chased me for most of my life. "I understand, believe it or not. But I also have my reasons to be afraid of you. You have threatened to kill me more than I can count."

I rolled my eyes. The hunter was wary of the prey. "I…" I didn't finish. I couldn't say I wouldn't kill him. It was the only card I had to keep this guy away from his malicious program. His self-preservation was the bug interrupting the flow of communication from the Cerebrander.

The one thing that programmed thoughts. Paul knew where it was. I hoped. It had been such a long shot. But he would take me there. And maybe, just maybe, I could reprogram it, like Molly did. I'd get a whole lot of Breathers on our side, including Paul. It would turn the tide of the upcoming war. It might even prevent it. My answer. The clue I needed. Maybe I could return to the future as a success.

"So, as long as I have information you need, I stay alive. If I tell you, what's the need for poor old Breather Paul anymore, especially since I'm already dying." Paul sounded a lot more sinister than before.

I was dealing with a Breather, my ultimate enemy. I needed him now. That was it. I couldn't push the issue too much.

Still… Drake didn't have the same, let's just say, "upbringing" that Paul did. "What was it like? Fifty years ago? When you were born?"

"Forty-five for me," he reminded. "I have five years left. Don't tell me I'm dead yet."

He sure took offense easily. Anything about his death. As I had seen in the future, he wanted to live more than anything else. And I had to be grateful for that.

"Okay, so?" The leaves crunched under my feet. It wasn't long until we reached the sub.

"I awoke with another Breather staring me in the face. We were enslaved. I had no mother. No father. I was carved out of a machine and put to work immediately. I was supposed to find Burners. I wasn't put into my mother's arms and cuddled like I've seen on all those television shows. I was running into a house and ripping a child out of its bed that very night."

How horrible. "Always children?"

Paul pushed a low-hanging branch out of his way. "Yeah. There weren't a lot of ways of finding out what they were until Cerebrander."

I held up my hand. We both paused. "You're telling me Cerebrander detects Burners?"

"It is an amazing piece of technology. The enemies of the Riders, my enemies, created a lot of machines that interacted with both body and mind. When they died, they utilized both."

Yeah, Paul was talking about what I needed from my friends now. The diaries. I should have known that the Cerebrander originated from the Simrulians. They were the only ones intent on keeping our planet from suffering the same way theirs did.

"Did you ever kill a Burner?" It just came out. I wanted to know, but I didn't want to know. Paul and I weren't friends. We were far from allies, but I needed him. I couldn't exactly feel the same way if I found out he watched a Burner die. Like Farrell did with Belinda…

"No. Not personally. I…was a caretaker, not an acquirer, at least not for long." Paul swayed into walking, and we journeyed on. "We have choices. We were given the rules and requirements as soon as we were born. I knew I'd be set free if I brought a certain number of Burners in. I could live anywhere in the world, waiting for my cue to strike."

I swallowed. My throat felt too tight. "Sounds good."

"But to do that, I'd have to hurt so many… You just don't understand. They were children. Tiny little things. Small fingers. Tiny faces who didn't know what I was doing. Sixteen-year-olds are drained and used as power. The young ones are just captured. At best, I was terrifying them. At worst, I was bringing them to their slaughter. I couldn't do it.

"I asked to become a caretaker, but even that wasn't right. I knew what happened. I saw them being taken. Their struggles. I didn't do anything personally. But it hurts!"

He clenched his fists as he swung his arms faster and faster. "You'll never know how much. I wanted to bring Burners in. I wanted them dead. But I just hated myself. Maybe it was a break in my programming."

I didn't agree, but I wouldn't respond. Farrell had also looked guilty at times. Paul had fought his programming because, at heart, he was a good Breather. Wow, who would have thought it?

"Over time, I got put in charge of the facility you freed. They were talking about retiring me because I hadn't gone out on the hunt for so long, and I hadn't graduated either. I was just there, content in staying as far away as possible from the death and suffering."

I remembered what Erin had said about Paul. "You bluffed."

He shot me a glance and kind of smiled. "Yeah. I scared the living daylights out of most of the kids. I wanted them to show the masters I wasn't worth retirement. My first act of rebellion. We're supposed to treat the kids right, to pretend that everything's one big happy home, but I made them all so nervous."

I had to laugh now. We reached the edge of the forest and just to the right, the submarine's shiny head stuck out of the water. How little did Paul know, he probably made Erin start training. In his own weird way, he gave them a reason to fight.

"Paul, look, you might be happy to see me again someday. You might even one day call me your friend. I hope so. Because…you are to be admired."

Paul snorted. "You are soft. I could rip your belly and let your guts fall out."

"Oh, scary," I mocked. We opened the submarine and slid in. Paul first. I didn't trust him that much, no matter his past.

He was still a Breather.

Breathers wanted me dead.

At least for a bit longer.

The Cerebrander might fix that. All I had to do was find it.

After we reached land, we had to leave the submarine far behind. Paul commandeered a car for us, and then he started driving. It was dangerous because he could easily cause a wreck and put me out of his hair for good. Still, I didn't think he'd risk himself.

Paul was a strange Breather. He was what he was born as, but there was a depth to him I hadn't realized before. He was good at technology. He found the stealth mode on the submarine and allowed it to hide in its deep underwater hiding place while we went on. I guess he planned to go back the way we came.

He also loved TV. He spent more time with that than with anything else. And when streaming services were invented, he died and went to heaven. As we drove, he filled me in on the intricacies of shows I had never watched. When I was young, the facility didn't allow outside entertainment. I had no clue why. Farrell had once said, "I don't want you getting ideas."

I was starting to understand why, as Paul told me about the plot of one show or another about overthrowing the tyrants who controlled the people. Sorry, Farrell, we had enough ideas on our own.

As we got closer to our destination, I suddenly had a flash of where we were going. And it wasn't good, not at all. Someone very vulnerable was there. Me. "The New York facility?" I asked, trying not to tell Paul what he could find there if we went—my unconscious body.

"Central HQ," Paul affirmed. "That's the place. It is the hub of all our activity. Molly, our former leader, had insisted that all business goes through there. The Cerebrander was hooked up the last time I checked."

I kept my mouth shut. It was funny that the place where Molly controlled the Breathers and the Flyers was the same as my one-hundred-year tomb. Well, not really funny…

I was rigid with worry. How could I keep Paul out of the basement? If he saw my form, helpless, his Breather evil would rise up. I knew that for certain.

"Where is the Cerebrander?" I asked. "Top floor?"

"Somewhere in the middle, I believe. It's kind of a strange device. It can't be too high in the sky, and it can't be too low." He didn't notice how tight I was. He was fiddling with the knobs on the radio, trying to bring music in.

But I forced myself to breathe. The middle. I could work with that. We had attacked and left the place in shambles. I hadn't seen it since I fell to my death. But if there was enough of a staircase left, we could grab the Cerebrander and get out. No need for him to know I was still there, floating and convalescing. I needed to stay there. What would happen if I couldn't be in that thing until I woke up a hundred years in the future? No helping Rust. No going back in time. No being here?

I shuddered.

Okay, *that* Paul noticed. "You cold? I thought Burners didn't get cold, especially ice ones."

I decided to be honest. He'd see past a lie. "The last time I was in that building, Molly attacked me. I guess I still have problems with that." *Killed me*, I added internally. Though, I was the one who killed myself. It still creeped me out.

"Gotcha. I don't understand that."

I looked at him, my eyebrow raised.

"Fear. That stuff that makes humans go crazy just because they are reminded of a past bad event."

I pursed my lips. "Don't Breathers feel fear?"

He nodded. "But not from past events. I don't shudder when I think of how close I got to death when you Burners attacked from the inside and almost killed me. I've been close to death hundreds of times but never let it affect my physical body."

I had to smile. "Never thought I'd say this, but I wish I had been born a Breather."

"And I, a Burner," he said quietly, looking off into the distance.

I believed him. This mission was to save my future, to save everyone. But some part of me warmed up to the idea of freeing any Breather who was forced into this life. Drake didn't have to worry about that. But Paul did.

Speaking of which… "Do you know Drake?"

Paul nodded.

I couldn't give too much information. "Did you know he was…different?"

Paul surprised me and nodded again. "There was an attack while he was being born. The place was rocked by some kind of energy that short-circuited the Cerebrander. But it went beyond with him. He had a choice."

I gaped at him. Paul caught it out of the corner of his eyes. "What?"

"It's just…you never exposed him. You knew he was…"

"A traitor, in certain words."

I nodded, though he was intent on the road.

"Yes, I did."

"But you never told on him! You allowed him to betray all of you!"

Paul grimaced. "I was never ordered to give secrets about Breathers. They aren't supposed to have any. I wouldn't ruin someone who got the very thing I have wished for my entire life."

My mind spun over this. If Paul had reported Drake, my sister would never have been born. My mom wouldn't be happy now. The little family that I barely knew wouldn't be happy.

I realized something. I trusted Paul. Scary.

The trip took a while longer. I hate to say it, but it was a pleasant one. Paul entertained me almost as much as if I myself had watched the shows he talked about. Soon, he was parking the car and we were walking toward the Central HQ.

Outside, the building looked undamaged. Paul looked into what appeared to be a rectangle light and said, "Molly." A red light scanned his eyes, and the door opened with a booming, "Security accepted."

We walked in, and the door closed behind us. "What would have happened if someone tried that who didn't belong?" I asked.

"Instant vaporization," Paul answered.

I laughed but stopped when I realized he was serious. Molly didn't screw around.

The place was still a mess. It seemed my friends had been busy fixing the many walkways around here. But the place where Molly had fallen was caved in. Her suit was still there, broken beyond moving, and without energy, it probably weighed a ton.

I looked up at the ceiling, but it had closed since I had flown in. This place didn't bring back the best of memories for me. Here, I had died. And in the future, it was in ruins.

"More problems?" Paul asked.

He didn't understand. I wouldn't try to make him. "Where is the Cerebrander?"

"Up this way. Oh, watch your step. There is shrapnel everywhere."

His concern was nice. I followed him, taking his advice. There were pieces of everything, from the building to Molly's suit, littered across the walkway that pointed up. Paul shoved some pieces out of the way, not caring when they fell to the bottom with loud clunks.

He reached the halfway and opened the door. No security here. Probably shorted out by my last display of electricity.

"In here."

I walked in. Paul let me go first. The Cerebrander had been here. "Had been" being the operative words. It was gone. There was only an empty hole with lots of tubes that had previously connected to the machinery. But the main thing, the Cerebrander I had come for, was gone. An empty hole mocked me for hoping.

"It's been moved," I said. "Where would it…?"

I was turning toward Paul when I saw the flash, the large piece of metal coming down onto my head.

Pain exploded behind my eyes. I wasn't even aware that I had fallen. Paul was over me.

CHAPTER 15

REDMOND

*W*e're here at the New York building we lost Laoni in. The two of them went inside. I had to steal a car to follow them, but my flame tracer did most of the work.

Now, I don't exactly know what to do. I can't go in the front way. The top is a bit time-consuming. I could probably burn my way in, but knowing Molly and her friends, something will stop me from doing that. Laoni's last attack had destroyed the inner security, but the outer still worked like a charm.

I'm standing outside, wondering what to do.

But I'm not too concerned. Laoni has gone to the side of the Breathers. They won't hurt her. I'm trying to tell myself that anyway. It's so hard to believe. What if they do? And do I even care? Should I?

This whole thing is a mess. More than a mess. It's a fire on top of burning dog doo in a stinky swamp surrounded by grotesque slimy nuclear waste! Does it sound like I'm freaking out, diary of mine? Well, good. Because I am!

Laoni, my Laoni. She is friends with a Breather. She willingly went with him, laughed with him. It makes my skin crawl. When she was dead, or presumed to be, I wanted to explode. When we left her alone in that fluid, wondering when she'd come back or if she would be okay, I wanted to create. I felt a little manic.

But now? Knowing that she has gone over to the dark side? I feel numb. Lost. Hopeless.

It's closer to where I was when Dad died. Right before I decided to run away. I didn't want Aunt Fonda asking what happened. I couldn't face her telling me she told me so. She had always been a beast about Dad's drinking. Lecturing, condemning. But the accident had only started with Dad.

It had ended with me and a fireball engulfing everything. I haven't really sat down and thought about it, so here goes. Nothing else to do while I wait, wondering when the traitor I still love will come out in tow with that Breather.

So, we were driving. Dad was sitting there, smiling his stupid grin, saying how good a driver he was. I remember now feeling... yeah, free. I was getting into the wild turns he was doing, imagining that instead of a drunken father bringing his son home from football practice, he was a race car driver showing his son the ropes so they both could race each other one day.

A fantasy. It got real pretty quick. He smashed into the side of that car, the passenger side door. The front crumpled into the woman, smashing her into the airbag. I had seen her face right before we hit. I remember screaming. Was it me? Or was it Dad? Or was it the little girl in the back seat? All I knew was that it looked okay before I smelled the gasoline. Both cars had stopped spinning. No worries about falling down an embankment. No other cars were coming. It was a quiet night.

Then that smell. Wrestling with my nose. I felt my spark hit it.

Dammit. It still hurts. Dad went up first, covered in alcohol as he was. His screams as he burned alive. Quickly. My flames gave him that mercy. But they didn't stop. My fire would never stop.

It took them all, eating hungrily as I stumbled out of the car.

This was what I thought she meant. Karen. My first love. She had once looked at me and said my attitude would bring me ruin. I had no clue what she meant. Okay, so I wasn't the funnest guy to be around. But I thought she understood. Of all people, with her own father always out for his fix. But she acted like I was a downer and dumped me.

But as I stared at the two burning cars, me being perfectly fine except for the burnt clothes on my back, I realized my attitude had brought me ruin. My fire had brought death. Running was all I had. Not that I had any real family other than Dad. They all tolerated me. They had hated Mom. I was a part of her. I can't count how often Aunt Fonda called me the unwanted mongrel.

I had nowhere to go, no one to turn to. And my fire just ate everything. Food started becoming morsels of charcoal. Sometimes I wondered if I was being burned from the inside out.

When I found my hideout, I just fell asleep. Until I couldn't take the confined place anymore. Until I couldn't take my own confined head anymore.

I sit here, watching the building I had left Laoni in, and I feel that same pain. My attitude will bring ruin.

But no! Laoni showed me how to hope! She couldn't have crossed over to the dark side. She would not be all burned and ugly the next time I see her, wearing a dark mask and telling me she's my father.

Okay, I'm being a little silly. But I don't believe it. I can't possibly believe it, because Laoni is my light. If Laoni goes dark, so do I. And I'm not dark. I'm still me.

The darkness I had been in before I saw her was absolute. I just knew I wanted it to end. I walked out of my hiding place, wondering if I should have gone home again first, if leaving a note would be responsible or pointless. Maybe a note to at least Aunt Fonda. Maybe Karen. She could at least have had the satisfaction of an "I told you so" as well.

But I told no one. I just walked, feeling my fire, knowing it was getting more and more dangerous. There had been nothing for me. I walked toward that bridge. I saw her. Falling.

I was floored. She was like a shooting star. Then she fell into the water—and ice! Amazing, powerful ice. I knew. I wasn't alone. There was a lamp in the darkness. And I ran toward her, a starving person on a dark night, seeing the light of a hotel or something.

Even though she brought Breathers into my life, my life was never as dark.

So, what is going on?

Possibilities. She's lying to Paul. No. She's good, but she's not that good.

Paul is a good guy. Nope. That guy is just a pain in my fire, not anything else.

Laoni is planning on killing him because he has my scent.

I honestly let that wash over me, Diary. It felt great that all these secrets were her trying to protect me. Because she loves me. Laoni does. I can feel it.

But problem! That makes no sense now. I'm not even sure she does love me anymore. She looks at me like she's terrified of me or something. As if she wants me as far away from her as possible.

The kiss she gave me on the island was...amazing. I almost felt whole again. Then she kidnapped the kids we saved, returned them to their vampire masters, went off with Paul, and is now inside with him doing...

What? Are they...lovers? Is he right now touching her, taking her clothes off? Are they inside laughing at stupid Redmond, who thought he was special to her?

No! Laoni isn't Karen. She would tell me if she was bored. She couldn't stay away from me long, even when she was dying, trying to protect me from it.

What else? Laoni is...wait. Laoni isn't Laoni?

Gotta stop for a second, Diary.

~~*

My mind has gone out of its, um, mind. The possibility that Laoni isn't Laoni has given me heartburn—if I could get heart-

burn. My inside feels hot. If she isn't Laoni, that would make complete sense. Could this Laoni be a fake?

Diary, I saw those Riders in their baby state. Melding with humanity, becoming human. The monster inside them looks completely benign when their human suits are on. That's how they take over. That means if Laoni were compromised, if they got her skin, it would have been simple to become her.

Argh! My mind really doesn't feel good. Not at all. If we left her helpless and a Rider got in there, we killed her.

That means that thing isn't Laoni. Now I'm scared—more than ever before. I guess I never believed that Laoni was dead.

She's dead. That's the truth, isn't it? Killed by a Rider. And that Rider is systematically destroying our resistance.

My mind is dead. It's gone. Maybe I am dark again. Maybe I'll go out. But first...

Diary, this is the second time I'm going to my death. But first, I need to make sure that Laoni isn't in that fluid. The Rider could just be a copy. I need to verify she's gone from her watery coffin.

But if she is, then that thing is dead. First, the Rider, then Paul. After that, me. Solve what went wrong when I met her. Maybe our love was too powerful to exist. Maybe we just need to stop, burn out. Maybe together, Laoni and I can exist in eternity with no pain, no Breathers. No darkness.

~~*

I'm back. It's been days since they went in. What is taking so long? I thought they'd be out by now. I have set up a little lookout place in a nearby car. Burned out to get in, but the owner can fix that. I watch. I wait. I write in this.

And I die. A little bit each day. There's nothing for me anymore. No island of peace. No friends. Nothing more than Laoni. Where she went. Why she doesn't talk to me. Why she sneaks around and confides in Rust more than me. The alien.

I want to get in. I need to check on Laoni! I can already see the building in my eyes. The path down to the basement. I can see her floating inside the liquid. But my eyes need to verify she's gone. I can't get in. I can't attack people who aren't leaving. What can I do? I thought I had this all sorted out. I'd follow, confront Laoni when she and Paul did something evil, and then find out whose side she was truly on. I didn't know I'd be stymied by a locked door, of all things. I didn't think I'd be left alone on my own so long my very dark ideas would become form, give me pain. Make me suffer.

Now, all I can do is think. Thinking is bad. It brings evil. I want to get in there. I need to get in there. All the answers are with the fake Laoni or that Augmenter she was in. It is my goal.

I am turning dark. Thoughts are coming so quickly. My mind is spinning out of...

Hey, wait! I have an idea! It's so clear. If Breathers are the only ones who can enter that building, then I need a Breather. Hey, I don't care if one has to die to get in. They'd kill me. I'm just preempting my defense.

Yes. I can get a Breather. I will get inside their impenetrable fortress. Wait here, Diary. I will be right back. Oh, and traitor Laoni, I'll get in, and then we'll talk. I'll show you what's it like to deal with a deranged and dark Redmond.

Diary, don't tell anyone this. If Laoni were good and alive, she'd never understand these thoughts. Keep it quiet. Keep it secret.

CHAPTER 16

My head hurt. My wrists ached. My stomach was empty and hollowed out. Something was in my mouth. Cloth. Memories came back in fragments. Paul had hit me. I had turned my back on him. Stupid!

I remained calm. Hadn't I been in worse places? At least this Breather had a soul of some sort. I just needed to bring back the fear of death for him.

My eyes flashed open to see Paul sitting in a chair across from me. I tried to move my hands, but I was shackled to the arms of a weird chair. I shook my head. With a flick of my fingers, I brought an ice dagger…

Nothing was happening! Just like before when I lost my powers! I was helpless!

"Don't bother," Paul said. "You were stupid to come here. This is Central HQ! All the tech we need is here, even the experimental chair that suppresses Burners' powers. Looks like it works pretty well. Don't you get it? You have no ice."

I tried to talk through the gag.

"Don't. I won't have your words changing my mind. I am

a Breather. That part of me is growing, learning. It wants to survive. You thought of me as a friend. I am not your friend!"

I managed to get my tongue under the cloth and spit it out of my mouth. My heart was pounding. This wasn't good. Not at all. I had no ice and Paul was giving in to the evil within. "Paul, you are my friend—."

He turned ravaged eyes toward me. "I'm going to kill you. That's my order."

"How long have you been debating that order?" I asked, trying to keep him talking. My hands hurt, the metal pressing me hard against the chair.

"Not debating!" he screamed. He sounded more and more unhinged. His other side was starting to show. "I was fighting. For six days now."

No. That statement freaked me out more than the dire situation I was in now. Six days. I was due to go back. Six days… I couldn't leave here without at least knowing where the Cerebrander was. I couldn't leave Paul alone here. If he explored…

"And I'm still alive," I tried. "I can't live long without food, water."

He nodded, proving my point. "I fed you. Forced it down. But only so I could take you to the higher-ups and get my reward."

I wouldn't believe that. "You can fight your programming. Let me go."

Paul's face turned into a snarl. "I can't do that."

"I want to free you. Don't you get that?" I had a flash of insight. "If I freed you, you could stay alive a lot longer. No more being forced to get into dangerous situations. You think my powers are gone, but they aren't. If you were free, I wouldn't have a reason to fight you. You wouldn't face death."

I smiled winningly, struggling a bit.

Paul looked like he was listening, albeit grudgingly. "Then why haven't you escaped?"

"Because I like you, Paul. You're such a cute guy."

Paul almost smiled. "I am a cute guy? I'm almost old enough to be your grandfather. You can't call me cute."

"Come on, Paul. You've fought for six days. Fight a little longer."

His face was crumpling, crunched up like a tin can and destroying any former essence. He drew a gun off the nearby table. I guessed it still worked. Paul would have made sure of it.

"Paul," I said, "look, there will be no end to your pain. Fight a little longer."

"Fight? Fight a tsunami with a spoon? A hurricane with a leaf? You had me when you could kill me. But now you're helpless. You're my enemy. I won't be able to take you anywhere without you fighting back. But right here, right now, I can kill you. I have to or you will kill me. You said so yourself."

No. The logic was working against me now.

He cocked the gun.

"Paul, no. I won't…Please…"

He pulled the trigger.

I closed my eyes.

~*~

Somehow, I was still here. I felt the chair under me. I could hear the sound of heavy breathing in the room—mine and Paul's. And someone else?

"Just hold it right there and maybe I won't kill you, Paul."

A voice of an angel. I was in heaven. Mond was here. He held his hand out, fire billowing out and surrounding him.

"Mond!" I said. "You followed me again?"

He flashed me…not a grin. He wasn't happy with me. What was he thinking?

"Mond…It's not…"

And Time reared its head again. No! The week was up. My body twisted and turned until I left the chair and flopped like a dead fish in front of Rust. He gave me a sad smile.

"Failed again, I see."

I had.

I let my eyes close as tears dripped down my cheeks.

CHAPTER 17

I was numb. Rust was being nice, almost too nice, but we both were disappointed. I had wasted so much time unconscious. I had turned my back on my enemy. It was just pure luck that Mond had been there.

Mond… The last look he gave me was a glare. And I had disappeared right in front of him. What must he think about me now?

"Here, hot chocolate." Rust pushed a warm thermos into my hands. I sipped at the creamy substance, letting it warm my stomach. Funny. I only had the ability to enjoy eating and drinking for a short time, and this was amazing. But I drank without really appreciating it.

"Don't worry," he added brightly. "We're getting closer. I can feel it. The war rages on, but soon we might…"

I snapped my neck to look at him. "War? What war?"

He smiled as if I were just being silly. "The war between the Imposters and the Breathers."

I squealed out loud. "There's a war? Right now? Being waged? Where's the battlefield? What are the stakes?"

A warm light roared through my head. This time, I hadn't

failed completely. The Breathers still lived. More, they were at war. The Imposters hadn't won completely.

"Uh, yes. The battlefield is far away, closer to the ocean. We're safe here. The stakes… I could swear I already told you this. I did, didn't I?" He put his thermos down and looked flummoxed. "Oh, I guess I didn't. Something you did changed the future. Please tell me it's a good thing."

I squealed again and hugged him, doing a little jig across the room and sloshing my hot chocolate in my cup. I had fully expected to come back and have everything the same. But I had changed things. "Which Breathers?"

Rust pursed his lips. He stood up and placed his hands behind his back. "The only ones left. I didn't think being out of the time loop would be so annoying. I expect you to know everything I do. My memories are being taken completely over. You don't know the Shadow Breathers?"

My mouth did strange things, tightening but still becoming completely loose as it hung open. "The Shadow Breathers are fighting? How'd that happen?"

"My understanding is they didn't know how the Burners were treated. When their kids were returned by a Burner…"

Me! I wanted to shriek, but I didn't want to interrupt.

"They went to check out the conditions of all the facilities. That's when we got a major ally on our side. Even with all the Burners dead, they still fight on."

That smoked the fire out of me. The Burners were still dead. I hadn't succeeded in the most important item on my agenda. Still, my heart was warmed. Small successes can do that.

"Okay, anything else I should know?" I asked.

Rust spread his hands and went to put his hot chocolate back in the sink. He didn't use the… Wait, where was the machine that made food?

I couldn't ask. Rust was continuing. "Only the fact that all the diaries are complete. We know everything my parents told me…"

"But how?" I asked. I hadn't gotten the chance to get Redmond to emote. I didn't even talk to him.

"Well, as Redmond was worried about you, he let out his emotions, and…"

I broke off his speech with my impromptu hug. I couldn't believe it. Redmond must have followed me and the worry he had… That was why he could save my life, why he was there. Then my face crumpled as I realized. He had seen me with Paul, allying with a Breather. How angry he must have felt. My stomach churned. I had betrayed him. But it had done the trick. Redmond had not lied in his diaries when he was worried about me being a traitor.

He had told the truth. I wondered what those diaries said. But Rust was looking at me like I was crazy. He had no idea how much this all meant.

"Redmond's diaries?"

Rust, ruffled, answered, "Well, yes. His were the details about where the ship was and how to get to it. Okay, enough." Rust maneuvered out of my hands. "That means nothing! We can't even reach the coordinates. There are way too many ships around it. Even if we managed to steal a ship, we'd be shot out of the sky before reaching the main ship. It's useless. I'm out of ideas."

I felt his despair. A fire was burning out every hope inside. But I wasn't so ready. Rust didn't know what I did. My small actions meant a war still raged. It was at least better than the desolate landscape that had greeted me the first time I woke up.

I walked toward the exit, letting my feet pound metallic thunks that echoed against the walls. The window showed something I never expected. The buildings were back. A little worse for wear, but standing tall. There were no people inside them. No one walked the streets. Cars were abandoned hulls. I could see clearly through the window; there was no fire around to mar my view.

But people were somewhere. There was a war now. Not just total failure.

"Rust," I said as he walked up next to me. I didn't look at him, but I saw his reflection in the window. Old, wrinkled. Green haired. "Is there still a place where the Imposters become humans? Are all humans just bodies for them now?'

Rust's reflection nodded.

Nothing big had changed, but a whole lot of small stuff did. Sometimes that's all you need for hope to burn again. My idea of the past seemed even better than before. The Shadow Breathers were fighting. They had never been controlled in the first place. But if I could get to the Cerebrander in the past, more than a war would wage. Maybe, just maybe, there would be a war we could win.

But the problem was the Cerebrander wasn't where Paul had shown me.

"He was lying to get you to a vulnerable place," Rust said as we sat down to a game of chess. I hated the game, but it distracted the hopeless Rust. I was trying to breathe it back into him, hope mouth-to-mouth, so to speak. But he wasn't taking it.

He moved his queen to steal my pawn. I didn't care. "No, I don't think he was," I said. "He was an ally until he realized it was gone and I couldn't save him. Then his evil took over. He fought!" I added to Rust's scoffing face. "For six days, he watched over my helpless body and he fought. He wasn't trying to trap me. The Cerebrander is somewhere, and Paul knows where it is. Or, well, he will now."

Rust stared at me from his side of the board. "Laoni, don't tell me you're thinking of doing what I think you're going to do."

"Oh, yeah, I am. Paul's out there, right?"

Rust nodded. "He just attacked us, remember?"

Good, so that hadn't changed. "Then he might know where Cerebrander was moved to. I get that machine, I turn off the evil switch, and we get so much more than just the Shadow Breathers. Look!"

Rust was drooping. He had no clue what to do next. Well, good thing for him, I did.

"If the Shadow Breathers alone could make a war and save this whole area, then imagine what a whole lot of them could do. When the invasion came, the Imposters wouldn't have Breather allies. We could turn the tides of history."

"Maybe." Rust sighed and rubbed his forehead. "Checkmate."

I glared at him. "Hey! I wasn't paying attention."

"That's war!" he spat. "You always have to pay attention or you'll lose your queen."

I got his point. But while his hope was dwindling, mine had caught hold again. I knew I was right. The Cerebrander was the key.

"Where is Paul?" I asked.

Rust stood up and walked to a closet. He opened it to show a row of guns, some big and silver, some small and compact. He gave me X-shaped straps to put on and then gently slid one of the large guns into place on my back. He did the same with another.

"He's around. But if you want to get to him, you'll have to go prepared to meet Neo Breather."

Oh, crap. I had hoped I'd never hear those words again. I never could go to sleep without seeing all those eyes. All that evil stuck in one place. "How do I use it?" I asked. "I've never played with a gun this big before."

"Simple—point and shoot. The energy keeps recharging. It can pack a wallop, though, so ground your feet and hold on tight. Trust me, you'd rather be thrown off your feet by a gun blowing a hole in a Neo Breather than have a hole taken out of you by one."

He slid the front door open, and we left again.

It was a lot different this time. Rubble made a long and expansive landscape. Now, there were a whole lot of alleys and hiding places. The buildings struck up into the sky. Empty and abandoned, but not alone.

Like when a storm is coming. It's quiet, but you know something awful is on the horizon.

"Keep a lookout. I look left. You look right." Rust wasn't goofing. He was an army commander. A leader. Someone who had lost troops before.

I did as he asked.

It was the noise that proved we weren't alone. Rubble falling, shifting feet.

And then...

"That thing isn't a Neo Breather!" I screamed as I grabbed for my gun.

It was at least as tall as a building. Way bigger than what I'd seen before. I didn't know if it had evolved or what, but now the multitude of arms, legs, and other body parts shoved together were encased in a steel-like skin. Its mouth unhinged and showed lots and lots of teeth.

Blazing eyes wriggled and moved.

I fired the gun without thinking.

A force of wind or energy or whatever pulled me backward as if I had just been hit by a car. I fell on my backside, scrambling back to try and keep an eye on the mutant Neo Breather.

Rust nailed a shot, but it sizzled harmlessly against the skin. I pressed my back against the ground and fired upward wildly.

I missed.

"Focus! Aim for the—"

Wherever I was supposed to aim for was lost as the Neo Breather reached down and swept its arm into Rust. He was propelled across the air. He froze for a second and then fell into a heap.

"Rust!" I fired wildly again.

The light beams flew past the Neo Breather, who sniffed the air. A hundred tongues fell out of its mouth and then, lingering, it licked its lips.

It wasn't after Rust.

"Burner smell. Need communion."

I so did not need communion. I stood up shakily, bracing my feet with ice, and then I fired again and again. I did not know where to aim, so I shot everywhere.

Blam! Its arms. Blam! Its elbows. Blam!

Its eyes! Yes! The light beam carved off a piece of its flesh and it moaned. It reached forward, a big bulking beast. Sinewy tendons, sharp bones. Its hand wrapped around me and I fired again and again.

But it blocked it.

Fingers made of millions of little fingers squeezed around me. Its mouth opened.

"Eat this, ugly!" I yelled and brought up a glacier, shoving it down its gullet.

To my surprise, it screamed.

"Still hungry?" I asked. Its fingers loosened as I shoved icicle after icicle down its throat.

I fell. I landed hard but managed to get to my feet in the same instant. The hand couldn't grasp me anymore. The ice I threw spread, freezing the Neo Breather where it stood.

Okay, that was strange.

I rushed over to Rust and checked his pulse. It was erratic and his eyes fluttered but didn't open.

"Rust, come on," I said. "You have to tell me what to do."

Rust's eyes snapped open. "I'm still here. What happened?"

"My most favorite ice sculpture," I said with a shaky laugh. "I don't get it. That thing is made up of Breathers. All my skills just are absorbed by them."

Rust walked forward and tapped its leg. I saw the Neo Breathers' multiple legs through the clear frozen stuff, not moving. Not alive.

"Laoni, you are the last Burner alive. No one could have known this."

"Known what?"

"The Neo Breather can't absorb anymore or it would have imploded. It's reached its limit. So, all it could do was freeze."

I tried to smile, but Rust's head was bleeding. I heard more noise. And I was just one Burner. I had a feeling there were lots of Neo Breathers out there.

"Let's go," I said. "We need to find Paul."

Rust turned and wobbled shakily. I gave him my arm, and he leaned heavily against me. I casually clicked my fingers and brought up an ice cast for his leg.

"Cold," he muttered. "But that feels good."

I smiled. "You just hold on, hear me? I need you."

Rust sighed. "I'm an old man. My ideas are gone. I thought for sure once we had the info my parents left, it'd help us. But everyone is gone. The past is where we can save the day. You take that info back in time with you and find that ship. Maybe then…"

The hopelessness still burned bright in his eyes. Rust had a broken leg. He was losing his energy. He was at the end of his life. But I got his point. The past Rust, the younger Rust, might be able to do something, but this one believed he was useless.

CHAPTER 18

e shuffled/walked toward the far end of town, keeping to the buildings' shadows. I wondered where Paul was. Did he have a home here? What had made him stay here?

As the buildings dwindled, I saw the place I had been in. The very place where Paul had knocked me out and almost killed me.

"Are you saying Paul's in there?" I demanded. How was that possible? Had he left my unconscious body alone all this time?

"Of course. It used to be the Central HQ for his kind. He likes staying there."

"But my body? How'd you get it out? When did I wake up…"

Rust gave me a quizzical eyebrow. "Um, Laoni, you appeared in front of me. Somehow, I knew that you were trying to save the past. But I didn't find you. You didn't wake up."

I froze. Another thing changed. I had left Paul alone where my body was. He had killed it.

I was… How was I alive? Time?

A whisper tugged at my brain. *Time touched until you're done.*

So…I was dead. If I didn't fix this, I'd be dead way before Redmond. I kept cheating death, didn't I?

I didn't waste any time knocking on Paul's door. I ripped it open with an ice battering ram.

I was no longer in the mood to play.

We found Paul easily. He looked the same as had the last time I had seen him in this future. Brown hair, goopy, Neo Breather eyes. He came out swinging. He must have been sure we would kill him. He wasn't too far wrong!

We exchanged fire, but he couldn't get past my ice shield. I had to remind myself I wasn't here for this. I needed the location of the Cerebrander, not vengeance.

I cut off the flow of my anger. "Paul! I'm not here to kill you."

His voice echoed from up above. I stared up the levels and saw him looking down. "You're not?"

"No. Come on out, and we'll talk. I promise."

Paul listened. Funny, he had been the man to kill me, and yet he trusted me. It seemed to take forever as he walked down toward us. Rust leaned against the wall. I gestured and pulled up an ice chair.

He sunk into it but gave me a wry smile. "I'm going to get hypothermia with any more help from you."

"You're welcome," I retorted, then looked at Paul. "Remember? What happened?"

He stared at me. Shadows upon shadows were on his face, taking his light away. "I do. You disappeared in front of me. Then that Fire Burner tried to kill me. We fought for so long. Then we made our way down to the basement. There you were, helpless."

A shudder went through me. That word was laced with two feelings—regret and victory.

"But you're still alive. I didn't kill you."

I wouldn't rid him of that notion! I walked forward, holding my hands out. I had no time for this. The minutes were marching on. Rust was injured. I was now living on borrowed time. I was really starting to hate this building. I had died here twice!

"I still need the Cerebrander," I said.

Paul's brow wrinkled as he lowered his weapon to swing at his hip. "Why? You do know it'd only help me? And they don't even use it anymore."

It was stupid. But what else could I do except tell the truth? I pulled up an ice chair for both of us.

"If I sit on that," Paul warned, "I'll draw your scent into me."

It didn't matter in this future. Nothing seemed to matter. "Sit. Breathe in. Come on. We're friends."

"Yeah. Where one friend murders the other." But he listened. He sat with a heavy sigh like he was an old man. I guess he was, no matter what he did to extend his life. "It's harder and harder to fight my evil these days."

"How are you still alive?" I asked. I knew what Rust said. I just wasn't sure how accurate it was.

"Breathers are born in something that takes DNA and combines it together. If taken and used properly, the viscous liquid in each tube can combine beings. I used it to draw one in with a reverse polarity charge. Long story."

Somehow, I didn't want the details. "And you've survived."

"It's what I do." His eyes took in the dingy and scuffed floor more than he looked at me. It was funny. As much as he wanted to survive, his actions now ran contrary to that desire. He wanted to die. "I don't want to know where the Cerebrander is now. I don't need it."

That was true. If I wanted to do something now, I could use our Journeyer, the copy of the Cerebrander. No. I needed the one in the past. A time when the Journeyer wasn't invented yet.

Or was it here now? My mind broke. All I could see was Rust putting his dish in the sink. No fire around the building. "The Journeyer," I asked Rust, surprising Paul by ignoring him. "Where is it?"

"Um, I don't know what you're talking about," he replied.

I grunted out a scream of frustration. Another change. My body died. Redmond would have defended it to the death. "You killed Redmond!" I yelled at Paul. I flung my ice forward and slit a cut in his cheek. "Didn't you?"

Paul yelped and fell out of his chair, but he slowly brought his gun up. I knocked it out of his hand with an ice missile and threw a giant hand of ice around him. Then I squeezed.

"Didn't you?" I screamed again.

Paul choked out a "Yes."

I gritted my teeth and squeezed. I didn't care how much Paul had fought his evil. I wanted him dead, gasping for breath as his heart exploded.

A gentle hand found my shoulder. "Laoni, you can change it."

I stopped, shaky breaths bursting through my lungs. Redmond had been killed defending me. I couldn't take it. His murderer was under my ice. I had to...

"Save Redmond. You have to save Redmond."

I dissolved the ice. I shook. Everything hurt. My eyes were blurred. "Where...where was the Cerebrander?" I asked Paul. "It wasn't in the place we checked. Where would it have been moved to?"

Paul was gaping at me. "You could have killed me! Why didn't you?"

"Tell me! Where is it?"

"Well, after…" He flinched as my hands clenched. "I was victorious. They like to honor the ones who have achieved major victories. My evil side liked that idea, so we… I traveled to the transport ship for a ceremony. I was going to get a house, a car, a job. I wanted it. I forgot everything."

"And that tells me where the stupid Cerebrander is?" I wanted to squeeze him again. Part of me didn't care that it wasn't his choice.

"It was on the main ship. Now, it's…"

"I don't care about now!" I yelled. "Where was it?"

"The transport ship," he repeated.

"Great! Goodbye." I turned and left, letting Rust lean against my shoulder. I couldn't stay any longer. Redmond was dead because of Paul. I wanted to return the favor.

But wasn't it more important to focus on life? On what could be, other than what was? Other than what had been caused by me?

Rust kept his eyes out for Paul or any Neo Breathers the whole way back. My own were blind, seeing Redmond fighting so hard to defend me. Having him slip into lifelessness. His eyes blank.

I knew he had died in this future. But it was a lot different being a hundred years in the future and knowing he had died at forty than knowing he died at seventeen because I had led him into a hopeless battle.

"We're back," Rust said.

I blinked to see that we were inside the building. A normal building. Not full of fire. None of Redmond's tech. I burst into tears, covering my mouth with my hand.

"Laoni, you already knew this. I told you…"

"Stop assuming what you told me!" I pushed my heels

into the floor. "I changed things, okay? You told me nothing. I'm aware of what I know. That's it."

Rust nodded. "Paul has your scent."

I rolled my eyes. "Not a problem. Trust me. The next time I go back, I'll either save him or kill him." I rubbed the wetness out of my eyes and out of my nose. I must have looked like a mess.

"So, you know where the main ship is. You have a plan to help us further. Is it all over? I mean, almost?"

I steepled my hands. "Yes. It is because I say so. Once we get the Breathers on our side, this war will be won. I just know it."

Rust collapsed. My ice cast held up, but he looked terrible.

"Rust, do you have anything for a broken leg? Medicine?"

Rust bit his lip. "I have a way of healing. But it's… Look, I don't want you to think less of me."

I was still raw with the grief of Redmond's death. It hurt too much to even wonder what Rust meant. "If you can fix yourself, then do it. Now."

I was ordering. When Rust had helped me, I listened to everything he said. But now I was falling more and more into my leader persona, where people listened to me and that was it.

"The thing is… We Simrulians are changers. We have a form we revert to in order to heal. But it would make me vulnerable. I couldn't risk it while Paul was out there."

"Heal yourself," I ordered again.

He nodded and then his whole body stiffened into a rigid board, his legs on the floor, his arms at his side, and his head on the back of the couch, like a Rust statue. He started rolling back and forth, and then…

Sploosh.

"Oh, Rust," I sighed. He turned into a giant slug. Well, not a slug. A watermelon-colored slimy thing, only rounder. His eyes still peered out, along with his facial features.

"I am gross to you, aren't I?" he asked.

I shot down my first responses. I knew better than to make someone feel bad just because I was grossed out. "No. But you look like a Neo Breather."

"You take that back!" he said.

"Okay, maybe not. A Breather in its womb?"

"I am taking offense now. Look, if you're referring to my, uh, body makeup, then it's only because the Imposters used our DNA to create new beings. I am the original. All Simrulians have two forms. My other one looks like the ones you Earthers have. But this is also my true form." Rust hummed his indignation.

I wanted to hurl. Instead, I got up and sat down next to him, leaning against all his slime. Funny, it was warm, and not sticky or gooey. "Rust, you're my family now. I don't want you ever to think I'm disgusted by you. So, please bear with me as I get used to this."

He leaned into me too. We sat there, Rust healing.

The truth was, Rust was still Rust. What did it matter what he looked like? He gave me his comfort, and I began to believe more and more in the idea that I could save Redmond—and me and everyone else.

It was Rust who had brought this hope, and Rust who kept rekindling it even when he had lost his.

It took three days for Rust to heal. When he morphed back into his more appealing form, his leg wasn't broken and he looked less terrible.

"Rust, you should have done that already. Never be afraid of showing who you are, at least not to me."

He grinned. His lips were still a little green. "I'll try to remember that."

There wasn't much to be done while we waited for Time

to take me again. I had the location, and I knew where I could find the Cerebrander. Now, I just had to do what I had to do.

As the minutes slowed to a crawl, I anticipated returning. I wanted to see Mond's face and make sure he was still alive. I sure hoped I didn't just kill Paul when I saw him again. I needed him.

I had a plan. If they gave a reward to Paul, we needed to make sure he had done something worthy. He couldn't kill me and definitely not Mond. So, the only thing that was left was to give him a new victory.

"You're going to hand yourself over to the bad guy?" Rust asked. We were standing at the window, watching Neo Breathers move across the empty city, no sign that they noticed us. And no sight of Paul.

"I think it's best," I said. "Paul got to go where the Cerebrander was in that time. That's where I have to be. I'll be okay. Trust me, they're not ready for a hundred-year augmented Burner."

"But…"

He couldn't convince me. I felt the touch of Time again. The buildings disappeared.

Slowly but surely, I appeared in front of Paul.

Then I formed an icy fist and punched him as hard as I could as Redmond gaped at me.

I was at the bottom of the Burner Augmenter. My form was obvious in the liquid. Recovering. And Redmond…

He was holding his fire up in the air,

He was going to attack me.

CHAPTER 19

REDMOND

I can't believe I am getting so comfortable writing in this thing. I just need somewhere for my thoughts to make sense. Here, they do.

Laoni... She disappeared in front of me. I mean, she was there one second, and the next, she was gone. She left me alone with that creepy Paul.

He had my scent. He had Laoni tied to a chair and was about to shoot her until I sent my fire at the bullet and gun, melting both.

Maybe Laoni wasn't a traitor after all. My mind is still spinning. Because it gets worse, way worse.

Paul and I, we fought our way through this place. I'm better than he thought. The time I dedicated to training has made me faster, stronger, better than a Breather. But Paul's good. He runs every time I get a weapon close enough to kill him. Really, he's nothing but a coward. He's like a cockroach. It's how he survives.

He headed down toward the basement.

This is the part where it gets weird. I don't know what else to think. Laoni is down here. She never left the Augmenter. Her hair is all black except for a few strands of white. She hasn't recovered, not like the Laoni I've seen. She's unconscious. She's still recovering.

Paul saw her too. His eyes lit up.

I am Laoni's guard dog now.

I've got a new explanation instead of the worst one I already thought of. Laoni somehow sent a psychic projection out of the Augmenter and is trying to save us all. She needs Paul for some reason, so she went and got him from the vampires.

It still doesn't make sense. I didn't know she could astral project. But then again, she can do many things I never imagined possible. It's at least a better explanation than that Laoni, my Laoni, is a traitor. And haven't I seen Nora and Natalie talk without being next to each other? Psychic powers have to exist on some level. And Laoni is the most powerful person I've ever known. Anything is possible with her.

Laoni must have used up all her strength, so now I have to defend her body.

Okay, yeah, sure, there are a whole lot of unknowns. Like, if she is a psychic projection, why not tell me? What goal could she possibly have if it ended with her still back in the Augmenter? Why was she being friendly with Paul? And why did Paul wait so long to kill her? Part of my brain tells me I'm being a moron. Laoni is not a psychic projection. It actually makes a lot more sense for her to be a traitor.

But how could she be? Paul is a maniac.

He's retreated for the time being, but he's not leaving. The dude has been really intent on living, staying alive, but now he's addicted. He looks at Laoni like she's his winning lottery ticket. He should be gone, but he keeps coming back. My fire does nothing, and he can move!

I'm... I have to admit it here. I wouldn't anywhere else. But I'm somewhat afraid. I think Paul might be the one who can kill me. He is agile, fast, and knows how to stay alive. He can eat all my fire and anything I can use against him, he dodges. Like insanely well.

I will protect Laoni. She's lost all her energy. Any psychic projection she had is gone now.

Paul wants to kill her. I can tell.

And so, our battle continues.

At least I'm with Laoni. The real Laoni. At least, what's left of her.

Redmond's fire was impressive. How had I gone so long without seeing its magnificence? Maybe because I usually was more intent on saving our lives than watching as his tendrils came at me.

"She's too weak!" he yelled and burned toward me. I threw up my ice shield, trying to let him wear himself out instead of hurting him. I wouldn't. He was alive now. I had stopped Paul.

"Redmond, please," I said. Paul was unconscious across the way, but he'd wake up. I didn't need to be fighting Redmond when he did. "It's me. Laoni."

"Then who is in there? Look at her!"

His fire made my ice appear red. I saw drips appearing. He was melting my shield.

I did as he asked. I had to admit it didn't look good. The Laoni of this time period was close to death. Her face was white. There was no energy in her. And Redmond knew I wasn't the real Laoni. Not the one he knew.

My ice shattered and he rushed me. I turned and ran, pounding up the stairs.

"Who are you?"

"I'm Laoni!" I yelped.

He caught me on the chin with a fire missile and I fell back to the floor. I caught myself by slipping ice under me.

I had to fight back. Redmond wouldn't listen to reason. He had been protecting my body for days. He was a warrior ready for anyone who came at me. Now, I was the one coming at me! He didn't care what I was. He was battling. That's all that mattered, a warrior fervor that didn't take logic as an explanation.

He jumped down. His fire leaped around him, curving in the stagnant air. It lit up my unconscious body and then slammed down next to me.

Redmond's eyes were crazed. I had to attack back, defend myself.

But I wouldn't. He thought I was an enemy, but I knew he wasn't mine. He was my moon.

He lifted his flame high, taking a piece of metal away from a machine and morphing it with his fire into a blade. Right in front of me, he was forging a sword to end the imposter's life.

My life.

"Cool," I whispered.

Now was the time to make my own blade, to at least slice his skin and stop his attempt at killing me. I had to. The future depended on it.

I didn't care. I was my own kind of warrior. If I fought now, it'd be to kill. And I wouldn't kill him. Mond was my future. I couldn't imagine turning my ice against him. It was only supposed to caress him, not hurt him.

Even if it cost my own life.

"You are some kind of Breather, aren't you?" he demanded, his eyes blazing. "Teaming up with a Breather to find Laoni and end her life. I won't let you."

He knelt down, his knee between my legs but not touching me. His blade raised.

"Any last words?" he asked, leaning down, his face inches from mine.

I was stupid. I should have fought back. Now the bleak future would come. Mond would probably die. They all would. But I wouldn't kill Mond. Ever.

"Yes," I said. "Come closer, please."

Mond brought his scowling lips close to mine. "Yes? What?"

"I love you," I said and kissed him. I put all my passion into it. I knocked my chin against his, bringing my hands up past his blade and wrapping them around his waist. Somehow, the world stopped existing. I was kissing Mond, and that's all that mattered. His skin on mine. His breath heavy. His fiery hot shoulders sizzling against my ice. Back in the same embrace that we always knew.

His blade clattered and fell, missing my face by inches. But all I did was pull him down. My ice dissolved. His fire left. His skin still felt hot under my touch as I explored his muscles.

We were only interrupted by our need for breath. Mond stared at me, his eyes burning a trail on my cheeks and lingering on my hair.

"You *are* Laoni. I don't understand."

Well, I couldn't explain it. "Oh, Mond. Um…" I racked my brain, trying to find a way to make this okay. "I'm a psychic projection from that Laoni."

Mond's eyebrows knitted together. "That's what I thought, but… She…" He pointed a strong finger toward the Augmenter. I reached up and pulled it to my lips, kissing it gently. He muttered and stroked my jaw. "There is no way that body is strong enough. She… You are still healing now. You can't…"

I knew he was right. My Mond was smart. "Okay, would you believe that I'm a multiple of her? A clone? A double who shares the same mind?"

"I'd find one of those hard to believe. But all three? Come on, Laoni."

He shifted off me, and I sat up. I held my knee to my chest as I stared at him.

"It's me," he continued. "I can tell when you're lying. So, don't. Not anymore. Tell me the truth."

"That's just it! I can't! I've got a secret. It is so big and so devastating, you can't know."

He blinked and nodded. "Well, okay. Then why didn't you just tell me that in the first place?"

I paused. Trying to keep my breath, I tried to explain. "Because…I didn't want to lie to you. This secret is bad. Life changing."

Mond visibly relaxed. He took a strand of my hair between his fingers and let it fall across his wrist. Its whiteness blazed a trail across his skin. "I believe that. You didn't have to tell me the secret. Just tell me what you can. Did you really think I'd hate you if you had a secret?"

Some part of me had. "Yeah. It's part of my upbringing, I guess. I was supposed to keep everything secret. You know, when my ice powers started. Secrets were the norm in the facility. Farrell kept many. I just thought that if I didn't tell you everything…"

Mond held my hand. He pulled it to his lips and breathed heavily into it. "It's okay, really. I don't need to know everything. That's what being in a relationship is about. Trusting the other enough to let them keep their secrets. Oh, Laoni. You don't know how relieved I am to…"

He glanced up at the unconscious Laoni, his lips pressed against my knuckles. "I don't need to know everything. Just ignore my question if you can't answer. But first. Is she you?"

I nodded.

"And you are truly you?"

I gave him a sly glance. "If not, you just cheated on me with me," I teased.

He actually laughed. Cool. "Okay. And this secret...do you need help?"

I bit my lip. "Yes. I do. But I don't..."

Mond held up his hand, mine still firmly entrenched in it. "Then tell everyone you have a secret and can't tell the details. All of us will understand. You don't know the turmoil you've caused on the island. Your mom. Gem. Natalie. They are all wondering if you came back...a little messed up from the Augmenter.

"And by now, they know you kidnapped those kids. Can you tell me why you did that, at least?"

I guess that wasn't a secret. "Mond, they didn't belong on our island. Their caretakers aren't harming them. We were the kidnappers in the first place. I just put them back. And you don't know how good that is."

Mond trusted me. I should have known he would. It would have saved me a whole lot of trouble if I had put faith in my guy and my friends.

"What's the plan?"

"The Breathers..." I glanced at Paul. Still unconscious. "None of them chose to live the way they do. Molly controlled all of them. And now, someone else is. Paul is a good man."

That was a little too much for Mond to believe. "Yes, a murderer. A real nice guy."

I reclaimed my hand and punched him on the shoulder. We both stood up and I leaned into his chest. This felt so right. I wished I had just told him from the beginning. So, a relationship could survive even with a secret. Good to know.

"Can you trust me on this too?" I asked. I gave him my

best set of soulful eyes, and he melted into me. It took another thirty minutes before we managed to get our lips away from each other.

"I'd follow you to the ends of the earth. Okay, so Paul is a nice guy. Are you saying all Breathers are?"

I wrinkled my nose. A Breather by the name of Digory hadn't looked too guilty when he was chasing us. "Not *all* of them. But right now, I know that every single one born has no choice whether to hunt us or not. I'd like to give them a choice. At the very least, a way of sorting out the good from the bad."

Mond stared at me. "You've changed, Laoni. Somehow. I can't put my finger on it. Like you've matured."

I was a hundred years older now. "Your imagination," I said easily. He caught the lie, but he quickly dismissed it like he had a feeling that my lies were the only thing that would save him.

"Okay, so what do we do?"

"I need Paul."

I slowly filled Mond in on what I planned to do. He agreed, except for one thing.

"Okay. Let's go back to the island now. We'll take Paul with us. Trust me, we'll deal with him so he can't use the info on the island's whereabouts against us."

I tried to interrupt, but Mond held his finger on my lower lip. I liked the pressure, so I shut up.

"You need allies. I would never let a Breather turn you over as a prisoner, which means Paul will turn both of us over. No offense to your importance, but I think the team that has been liberating Burners and the ones who killed a few of their higher-ups would be a better prize than just you."

"But—" I said around his finger. He stroked my lips, and I shut up again.

"You need all of us, Laoni. If this goes bad, we need a way out. I won't risk you. Not now." He stared at the almost-dead Laoni again. "I thought I lost you. Three times now. First, when Molly killed you. Second, when I thought you were a traitor. And third, when you disappeared in front of me. I won't risk it again. You going into an enemy's stronghold without a single one of your friends? No way. We'll keep Paul on ice for the time being."

Mond didn't mean what he said literally, but I encased Paul in an ice shell anyway. Let him absorb my scent. The next step was the end. I had to release him from his servitude or kill him. I couldn't let him come back here. Not with me here. Not when he could kill Mond, who would die for me.

"Okay, back to the island." I pulled Paul along. "I don't know what our friends will believe or not. I hope none of them want the full story. I just can't give that to them."

Mond's mouth was gaping at me, and then at Paul, and then at me again. "How? He didn't absorb your ice."

I shrugged. He didn't know how powerful I was now. "Would you believe I'm a super advanced cyborg clone of your previous girlfriend?"

Mond rolled his eyes. "Nice. Points for originality. I get the point. I'll stop asking questions."

Paul was an icicle on the roof of our vehicle as we left Central HQ. We left the weak me alone in that building with no defense. Mond was against it, but we had no choice. I trusted the fact that she'd…*I'd* be safe in there. After all, I had been for a hundred years. Nothing could hurt me.

I had more important things to do now. I had been safe before, and I would be now that we had Paul.

By the end of this, he'd be either our ally or our victim. We'd see.

CHAPTER 21

CINDY

*L*aoni is back! And I mean really back. She wasn't exactly fully here before. But she is now. I was really worried for a while there. It looked like Laoni...was a traitor! Shudder. I couldn't even begin to think it before. But I saw everyone's faces when they realized the kids were gone, along with the submarine and Redmond.

It was almost a funeral atmosphere, as if someone died! And it felt like it! Laoni was— Excuse me. Is our friend. Our hero. The one who liberated all of us. To think that she was a traitor had been devastating.

Erin was angry. I mean, mostly. Yeah, she also seemed a bit more smiley when I said out loud that I was worried Laoni wasn't the hero I thought she was. Like, whatever. Come on. Maybe I should stop praising Laoni so much. I've seen Erin get a sour face when I do.

I can take a hint! Erin doesn't like it. Well, hey, I'd praise Erin more if she'd let me. Every single time I tell her she's done something good, she tells me to shut up. How can I properly thank her for being in my life? I guess positive words, words of thanks, are one of my love languages. When someone tells me I did a good job, *my heart swells. I just want to make sure Erin feels the same way. What is her love language? I don't even know! She's not big on gifts, either. She does like spending time together. Like, not even doing anything. We don't have to talk or play a game. She seems happy just to be in the same room as me. Maybe that's enough for her. But how do I know she's happy if she doesn't tell me?*

Laoni is so, so, so much easier. She lets me sing her praises all day long. She doesn't love it, but she at least gives me a tight smile.

Oh, Erin, you are such a silly goose! But I'm glad Laoni's back and has given us...not an explanation, but a reason. It is about our survival. And the kids she kidnapped? They weren't even Burners. They belonged where they were.

Again, she was being all heroic and stuff.

She brought back a Breather. She's keeping him frozen. Who would have thought that was possible? I certainly can't imagine doing that. I wanted to try, but Laoni told me that he might, even through her ice, be able to catch my scent. For some reason, she doesn't mind if he has hers.

The plan! Oh my gosh! The plan is so amazing. This is why I think Laoni is amazing. She thinks that if she gets this thing called the Cerebrander, she can stop all Breathers from coming after us.

That means no more running. No more island.

I can see where my parents are. I can... I try not to think about them. A long time ago, I decided to be an optimistic person. If you look at the bad too much, it will bury you. So, I ignored the hope that I could maybe one day go back to my parents. I don't know if they'd accept me. I'm so much older now. I wasn't very old when I was taken. Did they have another child and move on? Will I ever dare find out?

But if the Breathers weren't trying to kill us every five seconds, I could go home. To dirty Los Lunas. Funny, I miss the dust. I miss Mom trying to grow the weeping willows in that dry soil only to cry when they died.

There's a lot I miss.

No, I don't! My life is here. I am happy.
Still, it would be nice...to be normal again.

I leaned against Mom's shoulder, breathing in her scent, watching Gem and Drake splash in the ocean surf. Mom was distracted by her boyfriend's perfect bod in his tight shorts. But she still kissed my forehead from time to time and squeezed my hand.

They all wanted to know what was going on. I knew now why I had kept it secret that I even had a secret. It was so much harder to relate with them knowing what happened in the future. Knowing there wasn't a legacy. No grandkids for Mom. Nothing left except a scorched earth and lots of human slaves.

Mond was on my other side. He kept a respectful distance. Mom wasn't sure about our relationship yet. She called it too serious. She had no idea how serious my life was. But his fingers inched over and touched my leg from time to time, leaving a trail of warmth and then pulling away before Mom's eyes could glare at him.

I was wearing a blue bikini. The air was warm, and the sand heated under my legs. Erin had started up a barbecue, so its rich smoke wafted gently into my nose and down the coast. A seagull's cry above made me feel as if I was on a family vacation.

This was almost a perfect moment. A family moment that I'd never had before. Me and my boyfriend next to Mom and my stepfather with my younger sister.

A few minutes later, Drake wrangled us into a fake volleyball game. We used trees as a net and tossed a woven ball around.

Natalie and Nora were on one side, and they cheated. They used their psychic bond to give secret messages and beat us every single time.

I watched Natalie's blonde ponytail bounce around. She wanted, of course, to know the whole story. But I told her as much of the truth as I dared—that everything could end if she knew, and she dropped it. But even now, she was miffed. Like I was deliberately keeping her out.

Or maybe she was jealous of me and my mom getting to know each other. Natalie had been a mother figure to me for a short time. But what role did she play now that Mom was back and taking her role seriously?

Mom was overjoyed when she found out there was a plan to maybe go back to normal. She was already on my butt about college.

College! I never even wanted to go, and now she was talking brochures and my future.

Natalie agreed with her.

I couldn't even argue with them. If this worked, the other me would have a future. We all would.

"Game over!" Cindy yodeled. She pointed at me. "You are a great Burner but a lousy athlete."

I stuck my tongue out at her. Immature. So what? I was entitled to a little immaturity, wasn't I?

The days were winding down. We had to unthaw Paul soon and get moving. I'd disappear again otherwise, and nothing would change. Redmond had sworn he wouldn't let me go until I did this whole family thing. I spent a lot of time playing games, eating, and lazing about. That was hardly what I needed to be doing.

I needed to fight. I needed to get to the Cerebrander and change minds. I needed to somehow stop that ultimate enemy of all of us and eliminate the Imposters.

Instead, I played volleyball and miniature golf and watched the stars with Gem.

The nights were filled with Mond, and I showed him how much I had missed him. But I just felt more and more worried as I relaxed.

Rust and I talked when I could be sure no one was listening.

"Did you tell anyone what was going on?" I asked him, my legs swinging back and forth on the examination table. My numbers were still high, but this was the only privacy I could get.

"I didn't know what I could tell," he admitted, shining a light in my ears. "I knew you weren't a traitor. But you didn't let me in on why you were freeing the new kids. I just shut my mouth and hoped."

I bit my lip and looked at him. "How often do you...revert?"

He dropped his flashlight thing. "Excuse me?"

"You need to turn into something else to heal. Do you need to in general?"

Rust turned around and pressed both hands on the nearby silver counter, leaving handprints behind. "How did you know?"

"Future you. Broke your leg. I saw."

He breathed six short breaths and then turned around. "I've never shown anyone that before. I was the only alien left of my kind. I won't talk about it. Please respect that."

I hid a smile. My friend was embarrassed, so I changed the subject. "How do you feel about Natalie?"

Rust threw his hands up in the air. "I hate future selves. They no longer need the secrets, so they expose the past. I really hate me from the future."

I gave him a break and slipped off the table. "My advice? Tell her sooner rather than later. I still don't know how much time we have left. You have to seize the moment."

I left with him scowling at me. And I went back to worrying.

I left Rust's doctor hut and almost ran into Erin. She looked ready to talk. Inside, I was worried. But I still forced a smile.

"What can I do for you?" I asked. "But don't ask me to tell you what's going on. I told you, I can't."

Erin held up her hands. She worried her lips for a few moments before saying, "Don't include Cindy."

I started walking, and Erin followed. I was more than relieved she wasn't demanding stuff from me.

"You're going to turn us all over to the Riders. I don't want Cindy involved. I need to keep her safe. Okay? Just say you won't have her come along."

I knew that feeling well. "I gotcha. I'd do the same for Mond." But I knew he wouldn't listen. Would Cindy?

"You're different." Erin stared at me. "More the hero that Cindy sees. Even I can tell."

"I'm still me!" I said brightly. She got the point and dropped it. She spun around on her foot and walked away.

Finally, on the fifth day, I couldn't take it anymore. I called everyone together and pulled my Paul icicle out. Then, I melted him.

He blinked and gaped at all of us. Then he looked out the window of the cabin we were in and at the island. "So! This is why I couldn't find your scent," he told Redmond. "Smart.

Water blocks our noses. But now that I know, I'll easily be able to return and kill you all."

"Paul," I said before Redmond could reply with fists. "I need to get to the main ship, where they are holding the Cerebrander."

Paul's eyes widened. "I don't even know that. How do you?"

"Long story," I said quickly. I wasn't about to tell him he was the one who had let me in on that secret far in the future. "You would need a huge victory to be let in, right? There would be a special ceremony or something."

"There's no way you are going to just let me kill you," he said.

Redmond gave him a hard look. He wasn't the only one. None of my friends really believed the Breathers had no say in their evil.

"That is the only way they'd let me in. If the Cerebrander is indeed on the fathership, then—" he started.

"The fathership?" I asked.

Paul smirked. "The Riders are a bit shortsighted when it comes to names. The fathership is the main ship that goes back and forth between the mothership and Earth. The ceremony you are talking about will take place on the fathership. It will fly to the mothership, and I will get a commendation. Then I will take the fathership back to Earth, where I will be set free."

Until the invasion, I thought. Paul didn't know that part. A secret mental bomb that would go off and destroy all of us...

"You sound pretty sure of yourself," Natalie noted.

"We all know the reward," he said. "They are ingrained in our heads. Succeed enough, and you get peace. I gave up on peace a long time ago."

Natalie growled in the back of her throat. "I really dislike you. You sound...sincere."

Paul blinked once. I saw the evil in his eyes. "I am sincere. And when I say this, know I am the same. If I get a chance, I will put all of you in the machine."

I quickly brought his attention to me. "Paul, you don't have to put us in the machine. You will bring me, Redmond, Natalie, Bobby, and Erin in. We are the resistance. If we were to fall, the whole thing would fall. Once you hand us over, your life will be at peace. You don't have to kill any of us."

His whole face relaxed. The evil burnt like a candle, but I saw who Paul really was. He was a victim. The person he most hated was himself.

"If you work with us, you will be able to survive for a lot longer. We have you now, at our mercy. You can't absorb my ice. If you work with us, I won't freeze your heart. Deal?"

"Okay, but we'll have to go to Central HQ to get the message to the ones in charge."

"No funny business?" I made sure.

Paul nodded. I trusted him. The rest didn't. Mond kept a fiery piece of metal aimed at Paul even as I iced him over again.

Cindy glared at me.

"What?" I asked.

"Erin, Redmond, Natalie, Bobby, and you? What about me? I'm part of this too."

I cast a look toward Erin. She could explain that.

"I asked her to leave you out." Erin crossed her arms, ready for a fight. The rest of us excused ourselves, leaving the cabin behind.

Natalie stared at me. "Are you sure this is a good idea? If Paul betrays us…"

"Trust me," was all I could say. Natalie dropped it.

The minutes seemed to be set on fast-forward. It was aggravating. When I was waiting to come back, they moved like glaciers. But now, they were on a bullet train.

"So, how will this work?" Natalie asked. "We all go in handcuffs or something?"

"We take the submarine. Paul will contact someone to come pick us up at Central HQ in New York. Just so you know, my body is still there."

Natalie's eyes widened.

"When this is all over, you have got to tell me what this all is," she replied.

"Me first," Redmond interrupted.

Seconds later, Erin and Cindy walked out. Erin pursed her lips. Cindy looked triumphant. "We're all going."

I shook my head. I wondered how good I would have been at convincing Redmond to stay behind. Not very, I decided.

"You ready?" I asked my team.

Bobby punched his fist into his hands. Erin was still pursing her lips, but she nodded.

The rest were more subdued. They knew we'd be surrounded by enemies. If this didn't work, we were done.

But they didn't know that they were done anyway if I couldn't get to the Cerebrander.

This was it. The penultimate battle before I dealt with whoever was in charge now. Whoever was commanding the deaths that Paul was falling into.

Somehow, I knew I'd meet the main baddie when we got to the fathership.

It was time to move.

CHAPTER 23

The submarine was crowded. Not because it was a small area with a team of Burners and a frozen Breather, but because everyone knew I had some humongous secret I couldn't tell them.

They understood, sure, but I couldn't tell them the exact stakes. That got them good. The air was stagnant. Every time I walked through the submarine as we traveled toward New York, they gave me looks, trying to figure out how dire everything really was.

All I could do was walk on and avoid every gaze.

Only Mond trusted me completely. Nice to know.

Still, I was thrilled that Cindy was there to distract Erin, and that Rust had also come along. At the last minute before leaving, he jumped on board. He was armed with three guns.

Natalie lectured him about how they were supposed to be prisoners and that coming *armed* might send the wrong signal. Rust just lapped it up. Natalie couldn't tell. But I could. He liked her yelling at him. He liked annoying her so that her eyes lit up with some kind of passion. I had to admit, I hadn't seen this side of her yet, like she was finally feeling something she hadn't felt since her boyfriend died. Like me, he had become an Alternate Burner and had been used up by his own power, a fate I had avoided by luck and love.

I think Bobby felt left out a bit. There were two established couples on board and one burgeoning one. Lucky for him, we all were in mission mode.

But did it take forever to get to New York or what!

We had to steal another vehicle. We were getting too good at that, and we rumbled down the highway.

I stared at the passing scenery. I couldn't help thinking. This was going to work…right? The days were so close to ending. If I went back again and nothing had changed, I would go crazy. And this wasn't even a sure thing!

Yay, I would get the Breathers away from their control. But Digory hadn't fought as hard as Paul. Neither did Farrell, no matter how much it looked as if he loved us. He had given in. How many wanted to? How many didn't even care?

They were strange beings, created by malice and hatred, but all in all, they were just a bunch of Frankenstein's creations. Could they be good? Or were they bred for evil?

"You okay?" Mond asked, squeezing my hand. The pressure and warmth felt wonderful. Every time he did, though, there was a slight frown on his face. Like I wasn't really his Laoni. He sensed the years, the extra powers the Augmenter gave me. I couldn't even tell him why, or what I was worried about.

As hard as it had been to lie utterly, this was even harder in many ways. To have something that could ruin our world on the tip of my tongue and have to bite it back every time. I was alone in this, except for Rust, and even he wasn't really here. I would be going back to the future devastation, not him. Nor would I return to the future being saved.

Funny how quickly I rushed to the devastation.

I slipped my hand out of Mond's and looked out the window. Natalie was speeding again. She was anxious. Her control of the car was the only clue, but she had nearly gotten us arrested the last time she was upset while she drove.

I could guess what was bothering her. One of two things. Or maybe both. Me. My knowledge of the future. The fact that I wasn't going to her or even looking to her as a leader. Technically, I was older than her now. I had experiences she didn't. That bothered her. Since I met her, I looked toward her as my mentor. My motherly figure. But I wasn't in the market any longer. I couldn't even tell her I wasn't in the market for my own mother. I had moved beyond that.

I was on my own in this. I had no one. Not even Mond.

And, of course, the second reason Natalie was so upset was just supposition. Rust was taking my advice. He was showing her how he felt about her. Not in a logical, mature way, but an annoying schoolyard kind of way. He must not have had much experience with love before. I could tell. He had been fighting the Breathers in his own way for such a long time.

But Natalie was pleased in her own schoolyard way. I couldn't read her mind, but I knew guilt. She had watched her first love die in front of her, and now she was feeling something again. For someone who could be her enemy. She had no clue what I knew.

Unfortunately, this was no time for love.

I felt as if I'd soon have to play referee. I couldn't allow them the same leniency they would have had on almost any other mission. The thing was that we had always tried to keep it somewhat light on the way to any battle. But now…

I couldn't afford to lose this one.

Luckily for me and them, we made it to our destination without any trouble.

We were able to easily walk in the front door with the unthawed Paul, and he got to work sending a message with some of the equipment in the building.

Then he sat back and waited.

"How long before anyone notices?" I asked.

Everyone else was getting ready to play prisoner. Natalie had brought along handcuffs that had quick releases on them, and everyone was helping each other put them on. Rust held Natalie's wrists a bit longer than he should have, and the looks between them were heating up.

Maybe I shouldn't have put my nose in that business. I sure hoped it didn't distract them.

"Minutes. The fathership moves fast." Paul stared me down.

I gave him a smile, which I think freaked him out. "Behave. Soon you will be free."

Paul snorted. It was unnerving looking at him, knowing that just under the surface were two sides, one that could help and one that could hurt.

I felt the ship rather than saw it. It was outside, cloaked in some kind of invisibility. At least, I guessed it was. None of the Imposters would want the humans of Earth to know about a possible invasion before it was time.

All of a sudden, we were surrounded. Breathers mainly, but I saw a few Imposters. All held weapons pointed at us. They were everywhere, up and down the walkways and spread out on the second-floor area, looking down at us on the first-floor lobby.

"Which Breather has caught these Burners?" one questioned. Okay, so he was important. How dangerous had we been to make someone so high up take an interest?

"I caught them all. They're subdued and ready to be drained," Paul said, stepping forward. He grabbed my handcuffs and yanked me forward. His dual side showed. At first, he was gentle, then cruel.

"Why isn't she dead?" the leader asked.

"It's hard for me to die," I said.

He cocked his head and looked me over. "*You* are the Burner who has become a hero?"

"Yep." I gave him a grin. My destroyed future had given me the gift of fearlessness. Our doomed ending scared me; this Imposter didn't. I had met worse. He wasn't even very menacing. I knew underneath the human skin there was a creature of ugliness, but whatever human he had melded with didn't impress me.

A flabby neck and a weak jaw. Graying hair and a mustache that drooped. He wore normal slacks and a suit coat with a fancy red tie. He looked like an accountant's assistant!

"And who are you?" I asked.

He could see that I wasn't impressed. For some reason, that made him angry. "I am La'R-Gon. You'd call me an emperor in your words."

Oh wow. The big guy. The boss. The head that wore the crown. I hadn't realized I'd be put in front of the very person who ruined my life. I should have known. Rust was across the way, surrounded by three Breathers. But the expression on his face said it all. He knew this guy.

His parents knew this guy. Heck, his parents had fought this guy to the death. The first one to step foot on our soil and try to take it over.

"Tell me, how could one young girl defeat so many of my creations? I have seen planets crumble, civilizations destroyed. My name is cursed in the whole Borco'aa''s galaxy."

"Never heard of it. But you shouldn't have come to Earth."

He stepped back. "I don't understand. I won. You are a speck of sand in my eye that I will wipe out. Yet you look me in the eye."

I faked a yawn as best I could with handcuffs on. It was a show. This guy was dangerous. I saw the ego in his eyes. Right now, I was surprising him because he was used to being obeyed. Even Paul was looking at me like I was insane.

But I had learned a lot on the run. Farrell had taught me. The Riders… Imposters. They scared me, and they knew it. That gave them power over me. Farrell had *loved* seeing my fear, and had sought it out. I could still remember him letting me escape, letting me think I was free, only to come after me or send someone. I'd never let anyone know I was scared ever again.

And I was wrong. La'R-Gon scared me. He was the reason for my ultimate fear. He would win. Like Paul survived, La'R-Gon succeeded. With him in charge, it was no wonder my future was in tatters.

Anger roared up in La'R-Gon's eyes. "Who is this *child?*" he yelled.

Now I was angry. But a low whistle reminded me where I was, what I wanted. Mond was letting me know to cool it. I could figure out why. This was my mission. Something that I needed to do.

"I apologize," I said. "Please don't hurt me." It turned my stomach. I wouldn't show my fear, but now I was acting it.

All for the greater cause, I told myself.

"Oh, I *will* hurt you. Hurting humans is fun. They have half the strength we do." His eyes were inches from mine. I wouldn't look back. He grabbed my jaw and squeezed it. "But Burners, now they're dangerous, aren't they? You have ice." I roughly yanked his hand away from my chin, giving me a slight cheek burn.

"You have ice," he added to Natalie. "You have fire." Mond. "You, fire," he said to Erin. "Ice." Cindy. "Fire." Bobby.

He looked toward Rust. "What's the matter? Couldn't you get any of the others to join you?"

My ears jerked at that. Others?

Rust was pushed forward. La'R-Gon smiled at him. "I know who you are. You think you move in the shadows, but I know what you've done. You like a murderer as group leader?" he asked me.

Cindy laughed. "Ha! Natalie's group leader. Laoni is our hero. You're way off base, ugly."

He didn't even bother to look her way. It was becoming readily apparent he only looked at Burners as tools. Not worth his effort.

He pulled back and punched Rust hard in the stomach. The Breathers behind him let him fall to his knees with a groan. "Your parents are dead, boy!" he hissed into his ear. I felt my fists tightening. Ice engrossed my knuckles. I held myself back. This was for his future too.

"My parents gave their lives to make sure you had a bloody lip for the rest of yours," Rust said. His eyebrows were so knitted together with hatred, I could barely see their individual features. "You will never win as long as I'm alive."

La'R-Gon reached out and took Rust's neck in his hands and lifted him up. "You will always be alive, but yes, I will win. Because I don't dare kill you. Your parents' DNA gave birth to a whole lot of hij-uy'a for me."

Rust glared ever harder. I wondered what La'R-Gon had just called us.

"I will not kill you. I will always let you live, so you may see what your stupid parents tried to protect be completely destroyed. I'll never leave Earth. These people have taken over this planet. They have become the apex predator of this world. It's admirable. But they need to fall and become the bodies for us. With enough time, many of our females will be born. The Dedgarnons will own this planet. The Simrulians will have one last survivor left. And that will kill you."

"Hey, stupid," I said. I didn't want Rust hit again. "You must have mud in your ears or something. But as my good friend just told you, I am their hero. I have stopped your stupid invasion. I know exactly what you're trying to do. So stop talking and kill us already. You're very boring."

He stiffened and looked back at me, his mouth gaping again. He had no idea what to do with me. He had little to no respect for Earthers as it was, and for Burners even less, if that was possible.

But I was the only one looking him in the eye. I could have faked fear again—my real stuff had evaporated into pure hatred—or I could just be me.

I snapped my fingers and sent a sliver of ice into his cheek. He flinched and pulled it out, only to have another sent his way.

He pulled it out again, but he didn't let me do another. He finally thought of me as something more.

My mistake. He walked forward and slammed my head into the floor. I went out.

Darkness claimed me.

CHAPTER 24

Stupid…

It was the first thought I had upon waking. What if I had gone out for two days? I'd be back in the future. I was relieved to see four metal walls around me that I didn't recognize. Cindy was across from me. I heard a slight hum, and a feeling of being up high encased me.

"Cindy?"

"You are so stupid!" she said.

I laughed even though it hurt my head. "So much for being your hero."

"You are still my hero, but heroes can still screw up. You were stupid. Did you have to make him knock you out?" She threw her hands in the air.

"Where are we?" I had no time for this. "How long was I out?"

"About a half an hour."

I closed my eyes in cool relief. "What's happening?"

"Well, I think Paul's out there being celebrated. You made Large-ass, or whatever his name is, actually think you were a capable enemy."

I punched my fist into my hand. "Great! I am stupid!"

"No." Cindy pursed her lips. "I thought you were. But…"

I rolled my eyes. "I'm your hero."

"He was going to kill us all," she said. "Now he wants our deaths to be a ceremony. Our painful deaths. Maybe you were stupid."

"Stop the back and forth. You're going to give me whiplash." I looked around. We were alone in a small silver room with only one toilet and a door with no window. Two cot-like beds were sticking out of the wall. Cindy was on the one across from me. "Nice place."

"I hate it." Cindy frowned. "I want out."

"Where are we again?"

Cindy swung her legs on her little cot. "We're in the fathership. I hope Erin's okay."

My heart froze. "And Mond?"

"As far as I know, we're all going to die together."

I wasn't scared. This was where we had to be. On this ship was the Cerebrander. All I had to do was get to it. I rushed over to the door and formed an ice battering ram.

"Don't do it. Look."

Her voice sounded subdued. She was holding up her arm. An angry red welt went from wrist to neck. "Feedback. Any elements will cause a beam of energy to burn. I dodged it just in time. You'll die if you…" I heard a catch in her voice. This wasn't good. Cindy was always an optimist, annoyingly so. But now, she sounded like she was giving up.

"Oh, Cindy. No."

She shook her head. It was then that I noticed that her hair was gone. Just an inch of black stood out from her scalp.

"What happened?"

"Look at yours," she said. I felt my head. I, too, was shorn.

"He called us sheep. He wants us to be slaughtered, so he had us shorn. He treats us like animals. He wants to demean us as much as possible. I can't even imagine how bad our deaths will be."

Yep, hatred was strong with me. I leaped up and held Cindy's head to my shoulder. "Hey, don't give up. I am your hero, right? How can you think I'd let that happen? I'm going to find a way to stop it."

I looked around the tight area, my eyes slipping across the silver walls that went to the ceiling, which was way too close to our heads.

"Somehow," I added. It didn't look good. I thought I'd find a way to get free. I had forgotten about the advanced technology the Imposters had stolen from so many worlds.

I let Cindy cry as I tried to figure out what to do next.

CHAPTER 25

RUST

This is probably the one thousandth and one entry I've made in my logs since I was old enough to write. Never before have I felt so utterly helpless. As of yet, I see no pattern in my own diaries. You'd think my parents would have left the information I needed in my own head.

Maybe they had no choice. Or maybe they never had any faith that I would be able to continue their legacy. So far, I haven't done a very good job.

It's Laoni's plan to be trapped in the belly of the fathership, not mine. She says it's for the future. She hasn't given me much information because she doesn't want to ruin what little future is left. She's told me enough. Ultimate failure with only me left. No others.

Not even Natalie.

Of course, Laoni told me it is years and years in the future, so I guess I'd outlive my friends anyway. But it sounds so dire. I don't have much to hope for. All this lies on the shoulders of a seventeen-year-old teenager who, though she is wise beyond her years, is a bit naïve in how this will all turn out.

La'R-Gon looked me in the eye. That murdering hij-uy'a hit me. I could do nothing about it. I sit in this metal room with only Redmond for company and I want to die. I want everything to end.

What good have I done? This lifelong war. I was so young when Simrul exploded, but I still see pieces flashing through the endless black, reflecting the light of our two suns. Mom and Dad cheered. Bitterly, they hugged each other and said, "It's over. It's done. They're gone."

And then that stinking ship, rising over all the debris. The utter despair washing over them as they clutched each other. Dad slamming his hand on the deep space teleport button.

I remember them crying even as a shiny blue and green planet came into view on the screen. I thought it was hope. My young brain imagined that our world had magically come back together again.

Mom watched me, pointing and jumping in my childish excitement. "Our home," I bleated over and over again.

Mom hugged me to her, Dad too, and they wept.

Little did I know that our presence would bring the Dedgarnons to our new world. Little did I know my parents would give their lives trying to prevent the fate of our old home from happening to our new one.

They failed.

I failed.

It is all on me. Everything. Laoni told me I would survive. But I puzzle over how to continue on, knowing what I do. Laoni said she came back to stop the future invasion. But where am I now?

La'R-Gon will kill us all. No one can get out of his prison.

I truly detest this creature from whatever underworld he crawled out of. He still scares me to tell the truth. The sight of him on every viewscreen in Simrul—not looking as he does now, of course, but the stolen Simrulian body he had. His eyes, though, haven't changed. Cruel. Taking great pleasure in his own cruelty. His people don't wish to survive. They wish to conquer—painfully.

We are not lucky that he is controlling the Cerebrander now.

Laoni told me we were because Molly Larson was dead, and she was worse than La'R-Gon. But she couldn't be. That woman only wanted revenge.

La'R-Gon wants everything. Every single life here affected by him. Serving him. Living for the sole purpose of what he can get out of them. I can't impress on Laoni how doomed we all are.

I have sent us to our doom by not stopping Laoni before it was time. I was too consumed by Natalie. Here I am, a grown Simrulian taking romance advice from a child!

It is just... This is amusing. Redmond is interrupting my writing. He is mocking me to cover up his own fear. He hates being trapped. It is amusing because not long ago, we had teamed up, and I was the one interrupting his own journaling. Of course, he isn't aware that I am writing my log. It is internal, and all he sees is me sitting with my fingers on my head, rubbing the small bump that helps me record this.

I should try and comfort the lad. But I can't even remember my own humor. I try every day to laugh, long and hard, to show the world and whatever else is out there that I do not care that they have given me such a life. The Burner, Cindy, agrees with me. She has said it's better to laugh in the face of danger than cry. Otherwise, the force against you has won.

But I am in the unfortunate position of knowing that the forces against me have already won. La'R-Gon killed my parents. He is responsible for my people's deaths and my home world's destruction. He has thwarted me at every turn.

I still recall the treatment I received in the bowels of the Earth with them. La'R-Gon knows that I have lost. He mocked me about it. My ribs still hurt from where he hit me.

What else can he take from me?

This is why I have never tried to find a partner on Earth, why even though Natalie has thrilled my soul, I try to stay away from her. Because everything I touch turns to poison. I have destroyed lives. I wasn't even aware that there were so many lives hurt by

La'R-Gon while I continued another war, one my own parents hadn't been aware of.

No. I feel my heart turning to stone. There is no way out of this. So, I will comfort Redmond. I will laugh and joke. I will put the boy's heart at ease.

For tomorrow we all will die.

Might as well die laughing.

This ends my log.

CHAPTER 26

The never-ending hum of the powerful engine drove me crazy. It reminded me there was a clock on this. But there was no way of knowing how much time was passing. I did my best to comfort Cindy, but it was impossible. We had no idea if the rest were alive. All of them could have been executed.

This had been my *great* idea!

I didn't know what to do! I couldn't even write in my diaries to kind of work this out. They gave us nothing!

It was over.

All of it.

And as the room around me wriggled and changed, I screamed out. I didn't want to go back. Not if I hadn't even finished my main goal.

But Time wasn't a kind master.

I was back. There was no building. Just an empty, ravaged lot. No...

"No!" I yelled. "Time, I can't leave now. If..."

But what *if?* The enormity of what happened hit me. I

couldn't go back until a week later. That was the rule. A week later, and they'd all be dead.

My friends. Redmond. Rust. Everyone.

I sank to the ground, gaping, heaving. Hoping something would come out of my mouth so I wouldn't feel this poison in my stomach.

How could…

Why…

I couldn't…

Fragmented words, thoughts, and ideas flashed through my brain.

It was over. Even if I could go back, I wouldn't save anyone. Rust wasn't even here now.

All I saw was nothing. My world was gone. The sky was brown. Clouds the shape of heavy aluminum hung overhead. Dust rolled through. I saw no greenery.

Rust was dead. He had been killed on the ship. I hadn't saved them. I had been after the Cerebrander!

"It should have worked!"

But nothing answered me. No one. Not even Time.

I slammed my knees into the ground. I pounded the dirt. My closed fists were bloody by the time I stopped heaving and crying. No, I couldn't even cry. Like I was broken, my tears wouldn't come.

Because I couldn't accept this.

The only victory now would be to stop the Imposters. And who the hell cared?

No. It couldn't end like this.

"Time!" I screeched. "You'd better talk to me. TIME!"

I couldn't talk to Time. It hadn't even begun before it was completely over. I had a plan. It was going to work. I…

"Redmond! Mond!" He was dead. More than dead. Again, murdered by my stupidity.

I closed my eyes and listened to my mind. I'd talk to Time. I'd ask. I'd beg.

But I couldn't. The Journeyer wasn't here. Never even created.

Dust rolled over me. I opened my eyes and saw nothing. I'd be buried. Long dead before I could even go back. I wouldn't eat or drink. My body would do itself in. The fragility of humanity. I could just stop living.

I let myself be buried. I saw nothing but black. My mind wandered.

Unbidden, I thought of all the strange things I'd seen on the way to Time. What had it been? Just nonsense? Was that what life was? Nothing? Just a ticking clock until we all gave up? No meaning. No loving.

"No," I whispered through cracked lips. "Mond matters. He is still alive, somewhere in time."

I had to reach him. I couldn't let him die.

I had the power. I did. Hadn't I traveled to Time on my own?

Not even knowing what I was doing, but knowing I had no other choice, I shot all thoughts out into the world, into the sky, into the very cosmos around.

Even as my body was layered with dust, heavy and all-encompassing, I was no longer there. I was summoning my ice motorcycle again.

I was straddling it.

There were highways in time. I didn't care what controlled it. There were pathways. I had to find them.

I was going insane. Nothing of reality mattered anymore. What was up or what was down? What was logic or lack of logic? Bodies meant nothing. Where did the mind go when it died? It didn't just disappear, did it? Not that much energy.

Not that much love. Not that much passion. Mond and me, we went beyond life and reality.

I would reach him.

I started my ice motorcycle and drove into millions of eyes, with waterfalls as tears. I skidded my wheels across a highway of living bone.

I ignored Time, and all its rules.

I was going back.

Nothing would rip me and Mond apart. Nothing!

I turned the handlebars to get more power and shot into blackness.

My body was no longer heavy.

I felt my lips bleeding and my head hurt.

But I had something under me that wasn't dirt.

Metal. Cold.

And that hum…

The hum of the engine of the fathership!

I jumped up to see a long silver hallway.

I was back.

Without even knowing how I knew, I slammed an ice hammer into the nearby door.

I saw two sets of wide eyes. One was Rust, staring at me as if I was some kind of angel. And there was Redmond.

Mond! I was back. Only minutes after I had left.

"Yes!" I yodeled and rushed forward, grabbing Mond's head and pulling him into a kiss.

Then a siren started roaring. Flashing red lights.

They knew I had broken the door down.

"Oh well," I said through Redmond's lips. "I didn't finish what I came for here anyway."

Rust held up one finger. He wanted an explanation.

I didn't have one. I mean, yes, I *think* I just controlled Time somehow. Or I manipulated it. I don't know! I just knew this wasn't over. I had no time to think, no matter how much I had just said screw you to it.

"I'll explain later. Get ready to fight. I need to find the Cerebrander."

Breathers appeared, coming from both ends of the silver hallway.

We were trapped.

CHAPTER 27

I, of course, have been in much tighter spots. I mean, didn't I just bend time the way it shouldn't have gone?

Within an instant, I threw up two walls of ice, blocking the entrances to the long hallway. I could practically feel the Breathers on the other side throwing their hands against it, trying to draw it in. Good luck with that.

"Laoni!" Mond said. "What is going on?"

I had to catch my breath at his shorn head. I hadn't noticed it before. His face was so visible. I felt like I did long ago, when we first met, and I'd wanted to ask if he'd be mine forever. I wanted to ask him again. But I didn't say anything.

"What happened to you? You're filthy. Your hands are bleeding. Did La'R-Gon…?"

I couldn't answer except to squeeze his hand while my other one pulled back my ice and obliterated the doors that blocked my friends. Erin flew out, and she embraced Cindy. Bobby was walking out with Natalie. All of them had short hair, only slight scrub behind their ears. Well-defined beauty. I wasn't sure how La'R-Gon could deny our perfection, but he, above everyone else, was immune.

"What's next?" Erin demanded.

"She disappeared!" Cindy said, looking toward me. "Right in front of me. What, can you teleport now, too?"

I don't know what my face looked like, but Mond quickly interjected. "She's a telepathic projection from her body in New York."

Cindy rolled her eyes. "Give me a break."

Okay, so that wasn't a lie anyone would believe.

"Doesn't matter. I need to get to the Cerebrander. If I do, it might be enough to get these things off us," I said. "And the war will be aided."

"What war?" Natalie asked with a hard look at me.

Oops!

"Please!" I yelled. I couldn't risk anymore. I saw that future. I had almost accepted all of their deaths. I couldn't do it again.

Natalie seemed to get my point. "Fine. Let's do this. Laoni, get through if you can. Everyone else, give her cover. Attack with no mercy. If this works, Laoni will control them."

Oh boy, did she miss the mark or what? I decided not to correct her on that.

"And if it doesn't work?" Erin asked.

"Then we're doomed anyway," Natalie answered.

They stood shoulder to shoulder. I brought down my ice wall.

Almost immediately, we were swarmed.

But a good thing about enemies having weapons is that you can take them away. I threw my ice as a bunch of hooks, snagged the guns the Breathers carried, and tossed them to my friends.

Behind me, my second ice wall was breaking.

"Fire, fire!" Rust yelled.

The world became light and darkness. And I ran.

I slipped past bodies and ran out into a bigger area. It became a dome at the top. All around were elevators that took people to other areas of the ship. I guessed they went sideways, as well as up and down. But I had no idea which to take. And I really didn't want to be trapped in an elevator in an alien ship right now.

"To the left. Sixth floor back," a voice said next to my ear. I spun around and blocked a punch from… Who else? Paul.

"Hello," I said. "Nice of you to come and save us."

He made a grimace. "Couldn't get away. They just had to celebrate me. And the Imposter wine?" He gave an exaggerated chef's kiss. "Impeccable. Besides," he added with a grin, "I am not allowed to free you. Good thing you freed yourself. I have your scent. I knew where you were. Are you going to save me? Or am I doomed?"

I felt the sadness in his heart. Whatever celebration had happened, I could see Paul slipping away. His evil was taking over. He had nothing left to fight with.

"The sixth floor back, you say?" I asked.

"Follow me. Oh, and stay next to me. Danger in front of me? Bad. Danger behind? Worse."

I didn't have time for this. I pushed him in front of me, and he ran with his head craned back constantly to watch me as he pushed the button to the elevator. I felt rather than saw my ice wall break. The echoes of weapons shooting metal came from behind me. I tapped my foot, waiting. Of all things to wait for, an elevator!

"Aren't there any stairs?" I asked.

"If you want to take a year to get to the Cerebrander." Paul swayed on his feet, holding his hands behind him and whistling as if this was a normal workday.

"Any time!" I snapped at him.

The doors popped open.

La'R-Gon stood in front of me.

It's a credit to me and my upbringing that I barely even blinked before I dropped to the floor and slid under his feet. With one mighty kick to La'R-Gon's backside, I waved Paul inside and slammed the six button.

"Not that one! Six back!" Paul yelled and pushed another button. The doors closed just as La'R-Gon got to his feet. His hand reached out to grab the elevator…

But we were moving.

"Do you know anything about the Cerebrander?" I asked Paul.

"It takes a lot of mental control to use it. You need to talk to it."

Sounded a lot like the Journeyer. Piece of cake.

"I don't know how you're doing it," Paul noted as the elevator made its way through the ship's innards. Little windows were around the silver area, flashing interior walls and other areas. The ship was abuzz with activity, and I saw a whole lot of Breathers. I could easily tell the difference between Riders and Breathers now. I once thought they were all the same, but Breathers didn't have that same wrongness that Riders did.

Everything about them was wrong. They weren't human; they wore human suits. Breathers were living beings.

"You won't know. Maybe never."

I felt so rigid, I thought I'd break if I moved even a finger. "How much longer?" I asked.

"Ten minutes. But when we get there, you'll have to come out swinging."

I breathed heavily. "What's here?"

"Neo Breathers."

Ugh.

"Breathers, of course. A few more Riders."

I gagged.

I needed to calm myself down. I had nine minutes to go, and I needed to be ready, not terrified. I looked at Paul, at his younger face that looked old. I could see the years draining him. I remembered how he survived. "The Neo Breathers. How do they exist?"

"You created them," he said easily. "La'R-Gon had no idea that when they have that birthing solution around them, they can merge with each other, become more…" He trailed off. I saw the look in his eyes. His idea. Of using that crap to make himself live past his expiration date.

"And what is that solution?" I asked to distract him. "It's so strange."

Paul shrugged. "I'm not sure. I think it comes from the dead bodies of the Riders' first enemies. In that essence is some kind of mutation, so it works out well for monsters."

Just when I thought the Imposters couldn't get worse. I wondered about all of this. Did the Imposters have the ability to transform before or after they came to the Simrul world? Rust hadn't told me much, but some part of me told me that the Imposters had stolen much more than just their planet. They stole their very DNA.

"Our floor," Paul said cheerily.

"Can I count on you to watch my back, or will you kill me?" I asked.

"Nope," he answered.

"Very helpful!" I yelled and the doors slammed open. I threw ice everywhere. I froze the air. Some Imposters became statues, some were impaled. Snow started falling, making the shiny floor slippery.

The new area was set up for the Cerebrander. As I slammed my way forward, I saw it at the end of a very red carpet, attached to lots of circuitry and wires. Once again, I blocked a punch from Paul as I pinned a Rider to the ceiling with an ice pillar.

"Paul, I'm going to save you!"

His eyes were crazy. "*He* doesn't want to be saved. He cares about survival too."

Once again, Paul was an ice statue. From here on out, I was my own. What else was new?

But the Breathers were unconscious. The Riders were dead. I walked forward. How eerily quiet it was now!

Then I realized something…

There were no Neo Breathers. Had Paul been—

I was encased. Some kind of cool liquid inched its way inside my skin.

I looked down and saw a hand made up of a hundred others.

"*Hi*," the being behind the hand said. I was lifted far up into the air, over all the dead or silent bodies, to look into the face of a Neo Breather.

And I knew this one. The same one I had turned into a permanent statue in the future. Or had I? What future had changed?

"I've never had a burner in my belly."

I felt sick. The liquid was penetrating my skin, bonding to me. I pulled up an ice shield under the hand and pushed it away. It was like peeling away a sticky seat from bare skin.

"Leave me alone!" I yelled and put spikes into my ice. The Neo Breather screamed as it dropped me.

I fell and hit my head. Then I threw out my arm, throwing ice into the Neo Breather.

And it fizzled.

"We were breathers. Or don't you know what happens when you use your powers directly on us?"

It barreled into me. I changed my technique. I created an

icy sword and started cutting. Not the Neo Breather, but the floor. As I peeled up one edge, whoosh!

Like in an airplane, suddenly, everything was sucked out. Nothing pinned down was lost, but the Neo Breather wasn't pinned down.

It was sucked down. I held on as the wind pulled on me. Without thinking, I covered the hole with my ice, and everything was calm again. My skin was tight, icky feeling. I smelled like a Neo Breather.

But it didn't matter. There were still more things on board. Lots of Breathers. That La'R-Gon. He couldn't lose as long as he had control of all the Breathers.

I dragged my feet over the frozen statues. The goop on my skin was disappearing. Thank goodness for small favors.

I was breathing hard, ready to sleep for a week.

But I went to the Cerebrander and stuck the mask over my face. It slipped into my brain. It didn't feel the same way as the Journeyer. It was wrong. Penetrating. Cold. But this time, it was connected to other minds. I wasn't alone. I was many.

Myriads. I felt Paul and his struggle. I knew where all the Breathers were, all across the world. Settling into homes, ready for one word from their owners to take over. The very end of our world started here, in this machine.

I should have just disconnected the minds from the machine. But Natalie knew me better than I knew myself. I had power. I couldn't risk... The Breathers couldn't be allowed to make bad choices.

I had no choice.

I let my love of Burners out through the channels. Through every mind there. I thought of Redmond. My true love. My rock and support. Of Natalie, my mother. My half-sister. Erin. Cindy. Everyone on our island. I thought of... me. How much I had lost.

I gave the Breathers knowledge of who we were.

Then I was done.

It was the best I could do.

Before I pulled the Cerebrander off my head, I snipped the connection. Every single one. No threads, no lines. No control.

Oh, and if *that* wasn't good enough, I destroyed the monster machine. I froze it and slammed my fist repeatedly into it.

How could I tell if it worked?

I stomped over to Paul.

I released him and watched his face.

He gaped at me. "How did you… I mean, I have to protect Burners. You put it in. I'm still controlled."

I couldn't feel guilty. "No choice. I had to make sure."

He gaped at me. I saw the awe in his eyes. He loved me. But he hated me. "You're no better than La'R-Gon or Molly. I still can't control my own feelings."

I opened my mouth to… I don't know, apologize?

But nothing came out. I had no chance. I was being pulled on again. By Time.

"Hey!" I screamed. "I haven't been here a week!"

But I could do nothing. As if I were caught in an ocean's current, I was yanked.

Time wanted to talk to me.

CHAPTER 28

I was getting used to insanity. Bleeding corn on the cob spiraling around me? No problem. Fuzzy anchors coming from old-fashioned sailing ships that smacked into my head as I was pulled along? I didn't care.

All that mattered was that this, whatever *this* was, ended quickly and I could go back. I mean, I think I settled the whole evil Breather thing, but I wasn't sure. And La'R-Gon was still a threat.

Somehow, after all my power recently, I couldn't quite let my control freak side go. I had to get back. To keep an eye on everything. And I had a week left, darn it!

Time didn't agree with me. I could tell it was angry. It was now a gigantic foxlike creature, all bared teeth and red fur.

"You take too much, mortal. Space warned me about you humans. Nothing is good enough. You demand everything even when we give you all we can."

I looked up into its eyes of stars. "I had to!" Its paw reached out and brought me closer, squeezing everything in me. "I don't care if you kill me! It was all over. I had no reason to survive if no one else did."

Time grumbled and roared, but its paws—and, more importantly, claws—loosened.

"It is done. Even I can't change that without causing more of a wound. You are forgiven."

Well, la dee dah! I looked up into its deep eyes as it set me down. "Time, how? I mean, did I really move through time?"

Time ate its own tail until it was reborn again, settling down with its nose between its paws. "Yes."

"Okay, then, how? I'm not a god. No immortal being. Am I…?"

I think Time laughed. But it was so hard to tell. "You are a human being. A mortal. The only power given to you is the one of ice. But your mortality is enough."

Okay, had no idea what that meant. "Care to elaborate?"

"The will of human beings is the most powerful thing in the universe. It can change the very fabric of space and time. But only if the being has a desire greater than one's own selfish wants and needs. Your will refused to give up on your friends and family, so you broke through my control and went back."

I remembered. That moment when I couldn't believe that my love for Mond was so easily eradicated. "Okay, great. I'll try not to do it again. Can you send me back? I still have a week. La'R-Gon won't give up."

Time squeezed the ground around me until all that was free was my head. "You are insufferable. That is the reason I don't communicate with mortals. They are egotistical and shortsighted. You caused a wound, human. I gave you the information. Every time you go back, you rip things apart. You didn't listen. Your need was more important. If you go back again, you will ruin the cosmos. Space and time will bleed into each other. No, you have to wait to go back."

I supposed as much. Damn it! I had wanted to see the look on La'R-Gon's face. Then something touched my brain. "But I can go back, right?"

The ground around me receded and I was able to stand. Or float. Or fly. I couldn't tell. I was upside down or inside out. Or normal. "You have reached the end of my favor. Taking what you want can only give you one more return. Otherwise, you will cause the ruination of not only your friends but every living thing, immortal or otherwise. Do you understand, simple mind?"

"Yeah, I got it," I retorted. And I did. But I wouldn't change anything. If I had waited a week this last time, La'R-Gon would have executed all my friends. I'd rip a hole in space and time large enough for a truck to drive through if that's what it took. But still...I got it. If I did any more damage, La'R-Gon wouldn't be the problem.

I would be—by killing everyone.

"Can I go back to the future now?" I asked.

"You may. Just make your promise. Give me your word that you will never attempt to break through time on your own again. Promise me, mortal, or you will never leave."

I almost laughed. As if I could be trusted.

"A promise to Time is a promise on the universe. Don't get any ideas about betraying it. If you promise, you are bound."

This was stupid. I was getting sick of talking to a fox. I was getting sick of *everything*. I would do what I had done again. Easily. But now I had to promise not to. "I promise I will never go back in time on my own again."

That was it. Suddenly, I was on my knees. A tiled floor was under me. I was back in the future. But devastation didn't greet me.

I had succeeded!

I breathed heavily. I looked around. No, this was unfamiliar. What had I messed up this time?

The building I was in now had nothing of Rust's style. Before, it was like a humongous house with a living room and other living spaces. Now, it kind of took my breath away.

I couldn't really explain if I tried. It just seemed like *home*. There were long white corridors with black framed pictures. Ceilings soared upward. The white walls were warm and friendly, covered in what looked like knitted blankets with pictures of people on them. I recognized them.

Erin and Natalie. Cindy. Bobby. They lined the hallway all the way to the end. The rugs, soft and warm and cushy, were about three feet away from each other.

I stood up slowly and walked, trailing the pictures with my fingers.

This wasn't Rust's fortress, the last defense of a ruined future.

Some part of me soared. It had worked. The invasion had ended. This was a memorial, not a defense.

And a hundred years later would be a perfect place for a memorial.

My heart soared but crashed at the same time. If it was over, then why was I still here? Alone?

The rest of the place was just as beautiful, leading up and up. A penthouse at the top. This place gave me no clue about what had happened. Every window was blocked by heavy curtains. As I climbed the stairs, I saw more and more I recognized. Not places or people, but of a person. This was Redmond's touch.

This was what he loved. Music played at a low tune over the whole area. I saw shelves and shelves of books, classics. Six or seven different copies of *Moby Dick*.

I had no reason or logic behind what I did next, but I yelled out loud, "Redmond! Mond! Are you here?"

I should have been calling out for Rust. This building could easily have been made by Mond in peacetime. He hadn't died at forty if there was no invasion, and he could have easily lived to a ripe old age.

But I just knew. I could almost feel his fire.

Sure enough, as I was halfway up the last staircase to the master bedroom, a head stuck out.

I blanched and backed up. It was a man with long white hair and a scruffy beard. It wasn't Rust.

"Laoni?" he whispered.

And I knew.

"Mond?"

I rushed up the stairs and tackled him. He went down with a moan but held onto me, tears flowing over his cheeks and into his beard.

"You're so old," I said, petting his wrinkles. His hair. I held him. But I was thrilled. He was alive.

"I knew it," he muttered, his lips touching my hair. "I knew you were time traveling."

I pulled back and framed his face with my hands. "You are too old. How can you be alive?"

I looked him over carefully to see any sign of Neo Breather enhancements. But it was just him, really, really old. I could barely recognize his handsome face inside the wrinkles.

"I had to stay alive until you came back. You disappeared right in front of Cindy. It was the same as with me. Then once the Breathers started *loving* us, I figured you would be there. But you weren't. You never came back."

His knee creaked and I gave him my shoulder. I wasn't used to caring for him, but I wouldn't let him be away from me. Not now. I had succeeded. There was a real chance I wouldn't be going back.

I helped him down the stairs, though he seemed agile enough. I couldn't help wondering what had happened to the rest even through all the feelings soaring through me. Did Mond live here on his own? And…what kind of relationship could we have now? It didn't matter, though. I was still alive, and Mond was too.

We settled down on a black loveseat that allowed me to cuddle up to him. It was fantastic. I could finally tell him everything.

"So, I went to New York. You were still there. I asked Rust, and he told me nothing. But he let me in on the fact that it'd take forty or fifty years for you to be healthy again. That's a long time. I figured it out."

His eyes were the same. Touched by sadness, but the same vibrant green. The sparkle was exploding there, and I could ignore all the wrinkles on his face. The snow-white hair that rivaled my own whiteness.

"Figured what out?" I asked, leaning my shoulder into his.

"If it would take fifty years for you to be able to get out of that Augmenter, then you couldn't possibly have been my Laoni. Somehow, you must have come from the future."

I scoffed. "And you figured that out just like that?"

"It makes for a great story," he said with a grin. I laughed. He was still Mond.

"So, you waited for me?" I asked. My heart felt way too big. I was still taken in by his expressive eyes.

"I had no choice. I would wait until the end of time for you."

His weathered hand stroked my face. I melted into him. It was all over. This was our future. His age didn't mean anything. "How did you stay alive so long?"

"I burned internally, recharging my cells."

I must have shown my confusion. Mond laughed and touched my eyebrow, marveling at it. "Remember? I could turn into pure flame. Natalie taught me. I learned more. It wears me out if I do it too long, but for those moments, my cells do not age. I spent years and years on fire, burning for you."

I closed my eyes and felt tears spurting out. "Natalie must have been thrilled to have you on the island. Or did everyone go back to living normally?"

He was silent. I looked at him. "You did live in peace after the Breathers thing, right?"

"Laoni, it wasn't your fault," he said. "No one could have known that La'R-Gon had a mental connection with his ship. We weren't ready for the mothership's attack."

Oh. I should have known even with all that was wrong now, it couldn't be that simple. I jumped up and shoved a heavy curtain away from the window. The sound of its creak and the dust that billowed upward told me how long it had been since this curtain was opened.

The same devastation I had come back to before spilled out from this solitary building. Dust was everywhere. Fire surrounded this building, burning anything that came close. What was worse was that even more alien ships patrolled the skies. Somehow, Mond was alive, alone in his building. He had survived, but I wasn't sure anything else had.

I had changed nothing.

CHAPTER 29

LAONI

Dear Diary,

I'm back, writing this in the future. I haven't felt much of the same need to write these days. Everything is go, go, go or wait, wait, wait. I can't seem to get my brain around it.

It turned out that our capture of La'R-Gon was premature because we didn't deal with the mothership. I knew Rust asked me for that info first and foremost, but I had forgotten. The problem with my life is when I solve one problem, I usually forget it and move on because there is always another problem.

This time, though, was the stupidest. I should have remembered the other ship, the one that Rust needed the coordinates of, because it needed destroying.

I feel sick. I only have one more chance to go back. I'm on day two. In only five more, I'll be back there, and somehow, I have to get to that ship and destroy it. I no longer know the coordinates. Rust isn't here.

Why, you ask? He died. Saving Natalie, who died quickly afterward. The mothership came down and sent a wave of energy across the planet. I should have known releasing their Breather slaves wouldn't go unnoticed. When that happened, La'R-Gon was through playing. I had been right in my summation of him. He did win. That's what he did.

I can't believe I can still cry even after all this pain, but I am. It only took a month to get La'R-Gon mad enough to attack. He summoned his ship and killed everyone who couldn't turn into fire.

Redmond survived. Not much else did. A few humans. Redmond tells me that the ones who have are still slowly but surely helping the Imposters be reborn, slower than before. La'R-Gon is still alive, of course. He was responsible for the explosion that decimated most of the world.

So many deaths are on my head.

And yet the disease called Imposters that runs rampant on this planet won't last long. La'R-Gon didn't get what he needed, so Redmond tells me there are plans to leave Earth again, to leave the devastation. If I were to stay in this future, Redmond and I would be alone. All of the humans who are left would go with the Imposters. A victory. I saved Earth just to destroy everyone on it. Somehow, I'm not thrilled about that!

Redmond— I mean, Mond is still my lifeline. Being with him allows me to shut down and just remember our lives—as long as I don't think about the future. Mond will die sooner than later. He is so old, and I am still young. Seventeen. He looks ninety.

I can't...

No. I was going to say I can't do this anymore. But I have to focus on my last hurrah. I am going back one more time. I just need to try and remember where the mothership is, or maybe just execute La'R-Gon before he sends that signal. I don't know. I'll know when I'm in it again.

For now, I'm living with Mond, playing house. I pretend I'm just as old as he is and we're an old married couple, existing for each other's company. We cook meals, do the dishes, play card games. We talk about the old days. The really old days, when it was just the two of us in the tunnel. That seems like...not just a lifetime ago, but many lifetimes ago. Was life ever really just that simple?

It's hard because he sees me as a teenager. I see him as an old man. But when we close our eyes, we only see our hearts. And that's what's important.

Can I do this? Can I save the world that is so destined to die?

I wonder.

CHAPTER 30

"More orange juice?" Mond asked, limping a bit.

I leaped up. "Hey, let me get that."

He groaned. "No. Don't. It makes me feel like you're my granddaughter, intent on helping her grandfather. I can manage."

I bit my lip as he placed the juice in front of me. He had already made a huge breakfast. He had spent a long time building an indoor farm, like on the island, and harvested all his fruits and vegetables. I looked around at the empty place and wondered how truly alone he must have felt.

"You know," I said, sipping the juice, "I wanted to tell you all about my time travel. But..."

"You couldn't." He gave me a wrinkled smile. He had tied his white hair behind his head. Now, he had longer hair than I did. Mine was still cut shaved to my head. Mond had forgotten that part and had fingered it, saying, "What happened?"

I pretended that I had just cut it. He didn't need to be

reminded how desperate our lives were back then. How bad mine still was.

"I shouldn't have left you," Mond said. He sat down with a sigh and looked closely at my face. "I should have unhooked you from the Augmenter."

"I would have died. You know that."

He only had juice in front of him. He wasn't hungry much these days, he said. "But you woke up alone. This was all on you."

I looked into his eyes, and he stared back. Worlds disappeared and were made in that gaze. "I've missed you so much," he said. His voice broke, old and tired.

"You have no idea," I responded. "I've been in front of you so much, but I couldn't be with you. I keep thinking about our days together, how they were…hard, but it was good being on our own. Only worrying about our lives and futures, nothing else."

He cracked a smile. "You never only cared about you, no matter what you said. I always saw the shadows of your friends. Face it, Oni. You're a hero. That's what you are."

I quickly changed the subject. I hated that word. I didn't feel heroic at all. "So, what should I do? Can I kill La'R-Gon and finish it?"

He sunk down into his chair. "No, I don't think so. I think the ship would retaliate as soon as his life ended. That's not the way to stop it."

I groaned. "Then what is? I mean, he has a connection to his ship. If we kill him, it will attack. If we let him go, he'll figure out a way to use his resources to take over again. If we do nothing, this will happen." I gestured at the curtains, closed again. I didn't want to see the dead world around this building. "What's the answer?"

Mond smiled.

"What?"

"You. I love you. I didn't know how I'd feel after all these years. I'm old enough to be your great-grandfather, and yet, when you talk, I'm a teenager again. You're my Oni. My girl."

I took his hand across the table. I felt the same about him. When he smiled, when we talked, he was my Mond. My guy. "We can't just stay here. Even if we wanted to."

Mond grew serious. "But maybe we could. I mean, we can live a while here. Food is no problem. No ship even comes close to this fire. We've agreed on an armistice forever. More of a standstill."

I gaped at him. "What are you saying? I don't have any control over the time thing."

He shook his head roughly. "You do. You forced yourself to go back to minutes after you left to save us all. You could talk to Time or just hold here. I know you could."

I sighed. I pushed my glass around on the clear table under me, leaving a trail of water, which I turned to ice. Then I drew pictures in it with my finger. "Maybe I could. But I have to fix this."

Silence filled the room. It was far from comfortable.

"Mond?" I asked. "What are you thinking?"

"It's just… Maybe we can't fix this. I've lived without you for so long. The only thing that withstood the blast from the mothership was my fire and the Augmenter, protected by the very thing helping you recover.

"Everyone else died. But think… Everyone has always died around us. My father. Those people he hit with the car. The woman you told me about when you were young. Our friends. And every single time you go back in time…"

He didn't finish. I knew what he was going to say. I made it worse. Or maybe not worse, but certainly not better. Rust had been the only survivor the first time. The second time was the same, but then Mond died a whole lot earlier. And again, when everyone died.

I wasn't saving the world. I was ruining it. "You're right," I agreed to his unspoken statement. "But what's the alternative?"

He reached out. "Like I said, stay here with me. Don't leave. What if you're lost in time? I have you back now. We could be together."

I compared his wrinkled hand to my smooth one. I looked into his weathered face and sighed. "But as what? You say I make you feel like a grandfather, but you're old, Mond."

He gave me a wry smile. "So, you can't be with me?"

"It's not fair!" I yelled. "We're supposed to both be at the cusp of our lives together. I wanted to celebrate when you turned eighteen. I had this whole surprise birthday party in mind because you gave me my gift. I wanted to see you grow older, slowly. Watch you try out different facial hair styles. Not that your hairy, old goat face isn't appealing," I teased, brushing his hair down to his shoulder.

"I know. I'm not what you want."

I closed my eyes and rushed around the table, holding his shoulder and leaning my head into his. He still smelled the same. He felt the same, but he was frail. Old. And who knew when the time he cheated would catch up to him. What if I agreed to stay and he died the next day? I didn't think I could face a century without him the way he had without me.

"Mond, I have to try at least one more time. For you. If there was no way back, I'd live here happily with you. We'd catch up on all the movies we missed while we were on the run. We'd learn to cook and make different dishes. I'd even give *Moby Dick* another try and then we could talk about it. But I have one more shot. Just one. I won't give up."

"Why, though?" Mond asked. He squeezed my waist, and I felt the tears in his eyes. "I'll lose you. What if you don't come back? Will this timeline run on? Will I be alone until I die? I don't want to risk that. The years without you... I lost everyone. But as long as I knew you could come back, I was okay. I can't lose you permanently."

I just held him. He knew my decision. At one time, I had tried to run out on my friends and live only for myself. But Mond had gotten me to go back. He had made me see that I was responsible for them all now. I had to make sure they all had a chance for a future.

And I was selfish. I wanted to be the one to discover Mond's first gray hair by running my fingers through it. I wanted us to marry and see if I passed on the ice gene if we had kids. I wanted that whole life.

This wasn't what I'd choose. I had to believe that even if I failed again, his life would freeze, and only seconds later, I'd return and then we'd see what the future could be.

But I hadn't given up. By sheer force of will, I had made myself go and save all of them. I'd do it again.

"Okay," Mond said. "You'll go back."

I slid away, and we headed toward the living room. We would rest this week, watching movies, until I was pulled back.

"I can't believe freeing the Breathers could cause such a world," I said as we settled down, Mond's head on my shoulder.

"Yeah. Such power. I'm glad you destroyed the Cerebrander. With that much power, La'R-Gon himself could have killed all the Breathers. I'm not sure if that would have been better or worse."

I froze. I had seen the coordinates of the ship. I knew…or I could find it. In the same way I sent that message to the Breathers, could I use it as an attack?

The Cerebrander was gone. But when I returned, Mond would be at the prime of his life. He could make the Journeyer earlier.

"Mond!" I yelled. "I think I know what to do. We're going to save them."

I looked over at Mond, but he wasn't moving.

"Mond?" I asked. But I couldn't hear any breath.

His face was calm, a smile on his old lips.

"Mond!" I yelled again, pushing him.

But whatever life was in him was gone.

Again, Mond died.

CHAPTER 31

I didn't bury the body. I couldn't. I spent the rest of the time avoiding that room. This was the worst week yet. My heart was frozen again. I was frozen. But as the seconds marched onto minutes, I realized everything was frozen.

I missed Mond. He died right next to me.

But he had already died. If the invasion hadn't happened, I would have still lost Mond. I wandered one small area, the hallway where my friends were memorialized. I slept there, barely eating, only to keep up my strength.

I searched my feelings, wondering where they had gone. Was it possible that I had lost more than time? Could I have lost myself?

As I waited and waited for that feeling of being dragged back, I worked up my plan and thought nonstop about Mond. His body, decaying on the couch where he died.

It took a while to realize that I was in mourning. Not just for Mond. And it wasn't for the recent death, but for the first. I had been in a state of shock since I found myself lost. I had died. That's what I thought had to happen.

And I had woken up to a world that wasn't mine. Since Rust told me everything, I had shut down. Feeling nothing. I was fueled by solving this problem.

So far, I didn't have the time to sit back and think. To really pay attention to the fact that I had lost everything. Mond dying on my shoulder nailed it in.

The idea I had wasn't enough to keep my mind off everything. I had lost. I had failed. Ultimately, I was failing all the time. And some of the last words spoken to me by Mond was that I couldn't succeed.

He had made an offer to live with me, to give up everything. And even *that* had failed. He was dead. And I was alone.

Loneliness wrapped around me.

All I had was my next plan. The last one. If it didn't work, if it followed suit, then I was doomed. But maybe that was my destiny. Maybe since it already happened, I couldn't change the past.

I stood, walked, paced, sat, and thought. Imagined Mond being here. Talking to me.

But in the forefront of my brain was the plan. His idea of using the Cerebrander to make an attack was a good one. Maybe I could do as I had done with Time and make a mental ice attack. Burnout the mothership.

It was somewhat ironic that Mond's last words had given me the idea of how to save everyone. That was the main goal, right?

Not to save me. Not to save just Mond. But to save all of them. And, like Mond said, I was a hero. And heroes didn't have the right to cry or mourn. I had to finish this—or die trying.

Finally, the minutes ran down.

I welcomed the feeling of getting far away from this oversized coffin. From the body of the only guy I'd ever love.

I appeared right where I needed to be. I wondered if Time had some help from Space too. Was Time trying to help me? I wouldn't know. I only had one more chance.

I was surprised to find myself in the fathership. Breathers were walking around, but they were smiling. I had only experienced sinister smiles, but these were friendly.

One immediately spotted me and pushed a button on the silvery wall.

"Laoni is back."

That sent the place into a tizzy of epic proportions.

Natalie came first. "Are you going to tell me where you keep disappearing off to?" she asked.

I shook my head. "Never. What is this?"

Natalie had to laugh. Her hair was a little fuzzy, still extremely short from where it was cut. "Business first. Walk with me."

"To Redmond," I said quickly. I didn't have a lot of time to get the Journeyer going. Luckily for me, I could still see the Cerebrander in its pieces. Redmond could use it. He didn't have to start from scratch.

"He's…"

I nodded. I knew where he was. Mond was always smart. He had already figured out where I had gone off to. "On fire, I know. Just lead me to him."

Natalie sighed. She gestured toward a huge wall where a door slid open and then closed after we walked through.

"He's flying around outside the ship. This way to the airlock."

"Soooooo?" I hinted.

Natalie got it. "We're all here. The ship has an invisibility button. Cool, huh?"

I nodded. It was. But I didn't care. My heart hadn't unfrozen yet.

"Well, I figured we could either go back to the island

and figure out how to fit this unwieldy behemoth there, or we could use it to figure out what to do next. With the aid of the Breathers, this ship has been opened up to us. I decided to name it Phoenix. Reborn from the ashes to live again."

I tried very hard not to roll my eyes. I had to remind myself that Natalie had just come off a major victory. For the Breathers to finally be on our side was magic to her. She didn't know what I did, that all of this was pointless.

"We use it to look for more Burners. Or Breathers. It has a scanner too." The excitement shined under her voice. I almost wished I could share it with her. I would have, way back when. If it weren't for the future.

"Where is La'R-Gon?" I asked.

Natalie smirked. "Locked in the same prison he locked us in. Now, he is our prisoner. Oh, and his hair, too, seems to have gotten a lot shorter. Don't you just *love* life!"

I looked away. I shrunk away from the Breathers walking past, who greeted both of us. It looked like I had succeeded in one area at least. They didn't look nearly as fearsome. No more hunts. No more facilities.

"Okay, why aren't you happier? What aren't you telling me?"

It took everything in me to turn back to her with a smile on my face. Natalie didn't need to worry about this, or about how much our entire world was on the tip of a razor and could fall to either side.

"I spent a lifetime hiding from these things. It's hard to believe they just turned over a new leaf because of a machine."

Natalie sighed and stopped. Right behind her was another round silver door. But it was much more enclosed than other places and had an interior room with another opening. We must have been up pretty high. I guessed this inner door was to help against pressure in outer space or something.

"You're not all wrong," she agreed. "A lot of them, well, actually liked their evil. We had to imprison quite a few. Just like Paul, who kind of played for both sides, we have a few who are fighting the new order."

I held onto my knuckles, trying to remain happy-looking. "Where's Paul?"

"In prison."

I turned to look at her.

"It seems he doesn't like being controlled. Like you were supposed to just set them free. Yeah-freaking-right, am I right?"

I laughed. I had never seen Natalie look so free. It warmed a piece of my heart. Maybe I hadn't failed utterly. "And Nora? The people on the island?"

Natalie opened the door. "They're making plans to find everyone's relatives. There will be a whole lot of happy families soon."

I worried my lip. "And the fact that they are Burners?"

Natalie frowned. Her eyes were shiny with hope, no matter the expression on her face. "The ones that sold their kids aren't getting them back. The parents whose children were kidnapped will learn the truth when the Burner thinks it's time. We're keeping it secret for the time being. Just because Breathers aren't actively hunting us doesn't mean we want to show all our cards. And there are a few Breathers who aren't too happy.

"But without an active Breather scene and the leader imprisoned, life can start being normal. Normal! I haven't known or seen normal in years! It's so…"

Suddenly she hugged me and squeezed the life out of me. "Laoni, thank you. I had no idea how good you were. Thank you so much."

I nodded. I was still frozen. Maybe I'd unthaw when everything was over. But for now, I needed my iced-over heart. "You're welcome. I really need to talk to Redmond."

Natalie laughed and released me. "You are a tough cookie. Maybe you can lighten up a little once you can return home to your Mom's."

Not likely!

"How is my mom?"

"How else? Happy! She can go home. Her daughter doesn't have anything to fear anymore. Neither of them. Laoni, we've won!"

One more squeeze and she left me alone.

But we hadn't won. Not yet. Maybe not at all. Somewhere in the holds of this ship was La'R-Gon, plotting, waiting. He would send a destructive beam down and destroy everyone when he realized how much *he* had lost.

Everyone would die.

Again.

I opened the door and felt the cold. I wasn't cold, my ice just hummed in unison. All around the second exit were clouds. I peeked out and looked back and saw empty air. No ship. Invisible. It *was* cool.

"Redmond!" I shouted.

I wasn't surprised to see his flying fire roar toward me.

He tackled me through the door and we landed on the inner floor. His lips were on mine before he lost his flame. Lucky for him, I was very cold.

I responded like I was drowning and he was air. He had taken his last breaths on my shoulder. But he was alive. His shorn hair was tight against his expressive face. He kissed me up and down my chin toward my neck. His hands gripped me tight.

"You're back!" he yelled. "I didn't think you'd come back."

I hadn't. Before. Once again, the cause and effect of time

was realigned. We managed to sit up, but no matter how little time I had, the last time, I held onto him. I kissed him on his eyebrows. On his forehead. My hands explored every inch of his wonderfully young and *alive* body.

Finally, we fell apart, panting. "I was worried," he said simply. "Should we go to my room?"

I knew what he was thinking. And I would have. But there was no time. I didn't know how long it'd take for Redmond to build the Journeyer. All I knew was that he had once, by the age of forty. We had a week. Less than…

"Mond, how good are you with machines? Inventions?"

His eyebrows rose. He held my hand and jiggled it. "I used to take radios apart when I was little. But all I did was destroy them. I didn't fix them."

I smiled. Mond made it easier. With him, my heart was a little less frozen. "What if I asked you to mess with that Cerebrander and make it work again? It has enough pieces."

His face fell. "I'm no good at that kind of thing, really."

But I knew he was. He had to be. "Take a look at it. Please."

I tried to keep everything out of my head, but his quiet and aged face was still ingrained in my memory. A desperate-sounding moan came out at the end.

Mond took me seriously. "You need this? Or want this?"

"I…"

But I didn't have to answer. He pulled me to standing, and we headed back down the corridor.

Mond looked overwhelmed when he saw the Cerebrander. "I can't fix this. I don't even know what half these things are!"

It was too much I was putting on him. But I had no choice. We had no choice.

"Mond, you told me I was better than I thought I was. That no matter what I said about myself, it was wrong. I once considered myself a coward who abandoned her friends. You told me how wrong that was, and we went back.

"Well, it's my turn. You *can* do this. I know you can. Because you are better than you think you are. Don't ever let those negative thoughts dictate what you can and can't do. I *know* you can do this."

Funnily, I actually did. I mean, I hadn't listened to Rust too much when I first started this whole thing. I had no idea if Mond came up with the Journeyer at seventeen or years from now at thirty or even later. And even if he could copy the Cerebrander, did that really mean he could repair the existing machine and get it to me so I could use it for my ultimate goal?

But it didn't matter. I knew Mond like he knew me. He could do this. He would.

We sent the Breathers out of the room and left Mond alone to get to work.

But I had another goal. I was still numb. It came from fear. If this failed, La'R-Gon would attack everyone with a destructive beam. He'd do anything to free himself.

But, if he weren't trapped, then he'd have no reason to. His goal was still to use all the humans. He'd come up with a new plan if he wasn't a helpless prisoner on his own ship.

Which meant I had to have a failsafe plan. If I died, that was okay. But I had started this whole process because Rust had survived. Maybe he could find a way to save the day even if I failed—which, let's face it, I probably would.

That meant I had to free La'R-Gon.

There is, of course, some benefit to being a hero. Nothing you do is wrong, and if you say something, your wonderful worshippers will do anything you desire. Terrifying, but useful. I convinced Natalie to send him out on one of the escape pods. He was confused, to say the least. He looked from me to Natalie to our army of Breathers, who kind of wanted him dead, and said, "This changes nothing. I will have your planet."

Then he boarded the escape pod, glared at us, and the door shut over him. The last I saw of that monster, he was heading toward outer space. Probably to the mothership. Perfect.

If I succeeded, I'd kill him too. If I didn't, then he wouldn't get revenge. Maybe the others could at least survive a little longer if I failed.

I tried to have faith.

But it was hard. This was my last chance. A few days alone with Mond would have lifted my spirits, but he was hard at work, day and night. And I watched him, memorizing every detail of his body and face. I'd need it when I went into oblivion. Because if this worked—and I prayed it would—then I would still go back to the future. My whole life would dissolve, never having existed in the first place.

I wondered what would happen to this time's Laoni.

Her ending wouldn't be as happy. My ending could never be.

CHAPTER 32

The minutes slowed in the right place at the right time. I watched Mond trying to get the hang of rebuilding something I had destroyed so utterly. This wasn't the Journeyer he'd make with plenty of time. This was a slap-dash repair job by an unskilled engineer.

I watched his muscles clench under his rolled-up shirt. His biceps firming and softening. Everything happened in there. We slept, ate, and talked only in that area. No one had to be told how important this was. They could see it in my eyes. Everyone left us alone, and I enjoyed the company of the guy who might die.

His frustrated scream echoed out, and he stomped down the steps, throwing whatever tool he was using. "I can't do this!" he yelled. "I'm a loser."

I grinned, stood up, gave him a long kiss on the lips, and said the same thing I had the last three times he'd done this. "You can. Take a break and you'll feel better."

He scowled and fell on one of the chairs someone had brought in. Comfortable armchairs with fuzzy material, two with a table nearby. Natalie took such good care of us. "You have too much faith in me." He pouted.

I saw the familiar look in his eye. He'd always had a problem with pessimism. It broke my heart to see his face like this. Flat, lifeless. Like everything in the world was over because he had reached a bump in the road.

I never tired of convincing him he was wrong. It wasn't just because there was so much riding on this. It was because it was too wonderful to see the light returning to his face. The happiness. Making the clouds give way to the sun I knew he was.

"You haven't failed me yet," I said quietly. There it was, the little shine coming.

"But I might this time."

I gestured to the plate of fruits and vegetables. "Want me to feed you?'

He grinned and leaned back, opening his mouth. I lingered over his lips with a strawberry. That was sensual, but the carrots and celery were so crunchy we laughed as I popped them into his mouth.

I had missed this. Every time I came back, the minutes had worked against me, going faster than I could believe. But now, it was slow. I still had five more days, and each one took longer than the last. Time was supposed to fly when you were having fun, but almost as in respect to how serious this was, that wasn't happening. My whole world was Mond and our little honeymoon.

"Okay, back to work." He shot an insecure glance at me. "You sure I can do this?"

"Absolutely positive." He had no idea where I was getting my info, but he sure loved to hear it. He returned to being buried by electronics and wires.

I had no idea about the progress. I didn't much care

about all that stuff. The hours spread on slowly, like an endless sun over the desert.

On the third day, Redmond finally laughed out loud. His head popped up and he rushed over to grab my hands. "I did it! It wasn't hard at all. The wires communicate. Like a fire, you know."

I laughed. Electricity wasn't fire. I should know! When I had that power, it took away from me, but Mond gave everything back.

"Go on." I didn't ask if it was ready. I wouldn't put that on him. I held enough worries for the both of us. Best to let him tell me when it was ready.

"I got a connection. I know how those little tendrils go inside the mind."

I blinked. "The what?"

"Okay, look. The face mask, you see it?"

I saw it. I had felt it. But no tendrils. "Yes?"

"When skin contacts with it, it triggers these little worm-like…"

I'm sure he continued on and on about how the Cerebrander worked. But I didn't want to think that little worms had been in contact with my brain. I knew the whole thing was telepathic, but how it worked? So not interested!

Suddenly, Mond tapped my shoulder. "Okay, Oni, I can see you don't care."

"That's not true!" I said weakly.

He grinned and slid onto my chair with me, half his weight on the arm of the chair, the other half pressing against my leg and shoulder. "I'll just say that it will work. I think. I fixed the main connector." He got a soft look on his face and brushed my hairline, like he missed moving my long hair. "If only I could understand how to fix what was going on in there."

I settled into the chair more, letting him lean closer. "What's going on in here?"

"You've changed. When I first met you, I saw a similar look. Like you had given up on life."

I tried to smile. "You're not wrong. I was so sick of being hunted."

Mond caressed my jaw. I leaned into it, closing my eyes. "But even back then, you had hope. When you told me of what I thought to be an imaginary safe place, you believed. You had faith. But…"

My eyes flashed open. I kissed his thumb, trying to get his mind off this topic. He could tell something big had happened. He had already realized I was from the future. I wasn't sure about Time's rules. He had existed in both times. He might go onto the future I had seen him die in. Still, I worried. If he asked too many questions…

He let me take his thumb into my mouth, but he was only minorly distracted. I think he did that just to keep my mouth occupied. "You've given up," he whispered, a husky tone to his voice.

Okay, *that* wasn't what I expected. I pulled away from his thumb. "Given up? Not hardly. I can't."

"Yeah, yeah, you have. You have this defeated look in your eyes. Like you already expect my death."

He wasn't wrong. I had already experienced his death. In the future. Right in front of me.

I wrapped my arms around his waist and snuggled into his chest. "Okay. Yeah. I have. A bit. But let's just say my entire life hangs in the balance."

He stroked my head. "No, it doesn't."

I shook my head, but he caught it before I could go far.

"Not right now. Not here. I've learned something. The result of what happens? Yeah, that's something to either mourn or celebrate. But worrying about it or anticipating it does absolutely nothing. It's empty as dandelion fluff on the wind."

"But—" I said.

Again, he shushed me. "No, Oni, really. You've taught me this. I was so miserable in my cave after I killed those people. I condemned myself a million times. I lived in that moment. It may have been done in minutes, but I carried it with me forever. They say that time is relative. That things happen, and then they're gone. But it's not true. In my mind, it's always that wreck. My dad's face as the light went out. The bodies of the people he hit.

"Infinite and never-ending. But I can make it end in my mind. In reality, sure, they're gone. But in my mind, they are suffering again and again. After meeting you, after having something to fight for, I saw that I was no longer living those memories. They finally ended."

I mulled over what he said, silent as he kissed the top of my head. It was true. Technically, Mond hadn't even died yet. But he was already dead in my head. My own mind could travel through time, staying in one place forever, never letting it leave.

"But what if—?" I whispered.

"What if nothing. You have control over your mind. Whatever pain or suffering or worries you have, you can box them up and forget them. You've done it before. We have always been in danger. But you enjoyed life with me once. You sent your worries and fears away. I did too. You've been the difference, but I had to do it on my own. You've been popping in and out so often, it's easy for me to forget that your body is still in the New York Augmenter, practically dying."

I bit my lip, but he didn't stay on that.

"But before you came back, I was a mess. I helped no one. I only thought about how I could go back. I didn't care about my friends. Or…anything. But that was on me. Not the events. I realized that even if you came back, if I lived long enough in that misery, I'd be transformed. I didn't want that. So, I looked on the bright side.

"Outside, Oni, you can't change a thing."

How little he knew!

"But inside your mind is your house. Now…"

"My house is vacant and abandoned."

He nodded and pulled away to stare into my eyes. He held my chin and tilted it up. "Yeah. I guess so. And I hate it."

"Me too," I responded. Mond gave me another kiss and then jumped up to get back to work. He really was good at this. It was no wonder he had created so many things later. He loved it. It was his calling.

I wondered what mine was. Mond was right. I had allowed my history and life to paint my present. It wasn't Digory or Farrell or my father who sold me out. Those were just cutting the grass on my front lawn. I had let those events raze my house to the ground. Mentally speaking.

Mond could tell, even though he knew nothing else, that I had been devastated. He could tell it from my attitude, how I treated him. So, not only was I making myself miserable, I was hurting him too. I wouldn't choose that!

But how did I change it? How could I stop seeing Mond die in my mind? How could I forget the gnawing pain in my stomach that even now counted the minutes until I would be pulled back to the future?

Mond had done it. He had left me. To him, that had been the worst crime he'd ever committed. But he was still…happy.

Wow… I realized I wasn't.

That made all the difference.

I closed my eyes and forced myself to see something different from Mond's old face dying. Equal futures were possible right now. There was another one. I forced myself to see him dying again, but with me, the same age next to him, holding hands and surrounded by grandchildren.

As he worked, I asked what I wanted to be. I had a future. I just had to believe in it.

What would I want?

If life was normal. If I was like Natalie and believed this could all be fixed? When I grew up, what did I want to be?

I had never thought about it. Ever. I just wanted to grow up and be alive. Mom wanted something from me. College. That normal stuff. And what would that be like? What would I study?

It came to me in a flash. I guess there had been some thought over the years, a fantasy. Like the same kind of question as, "What would I do if I had a unicorn as a pet?" But it was there.

I wanted to be an artist. Not painting. I didn't like that much. It was too messy, and the wrong outfit would make me freeze all the paint. But sculpting. Like with my ice, but more permanent. Something I could show off, do an exhibit. I guess I did need college for that.

I was smiling as Mond took his next break.

"Well, hello there, old friend," he said with a grin. "I've missed you."

"I've missed me too," I admitted. "And you…"

My future flashed in my eyes again. This would work. It had to.

"So…?"

"I know how to fix it," he said with a smug smirk on his face.

I jumped up and grabbed hold of his hands.

He had done it! He was brilliant!

And we had time. I looked across the way to the Cerebrander, completely intact. Almost ready for me.

The next few days were wild. I felt more like myself than ever before. I smiled a lot and helped Mond with whatever he needed. Supplies were brought to us, but it was slow going. Time was a jerk! It sped up. The days flew by so fast. Okay, fine, I guess time did fly when you were having fun!

Because I was. I was back. Mond and I took turns reminding each other how to behave.

Finally! Mond jumped off the side of the platform attached to the Cerebrander and sighed. "That was hard. But it's done. You want me to take a test drive?"

I shook my head. "I've gotta do something. Then we have some plans to discuss. Like…where do you want to go to college?"

He laughed as I climbed the stairs to the Cerebrander.

Flashing red lights slammed through the area.

Natalie's voice echoed around us. "We are under attack. We're being boarded. All hands, be ready to fight."

The ship turned on its end, and I slid down away from the Cerebrander.

Only minutes later, I saw Riders climbing the floor, somehow holding on by magnetic boots.

They didn't look at me or Mond. They were heading toward the Cerebrander!

La'R-Gon wanted his control back. That was his main goal.

Everything was so loud. The alarms, the screams. Explosions rocked the ship inside and out.

I shot out my hand, creating icy steps to walk up the slanted floor toward the Riders. The ship seemed to be stabilizing, rocking and tilting, trying to regain its proper position.

All I could do was climb. This was another obstacle. *The* obstacle. If La'R-Gon retrieved it, this resistance was over. I knew what would happen then.

One of the Riders reached the Cerebrander.

With an inhuman howl, I launched myself across the bucking floor. I couldn't lose my only hope. I sure hoped the Rider grabbing the Cerebrander and unhooking its main parts wasn't as enthused by his mission.

I wouldn't fail.

As I tackled him, I caught him from the side, but he held on to the Cerebrander and stayed upright.

"Get off me!" he yelled, slamming his elbow into my head. The red shock hit me, but I held on. I brought my leg up from behind me to do an overhead kick. Adrenaline thrilled my bones, and I was in this.

I was gratified to hear him grunt in pain.

"Leave me alone!" he yelled, punching me right in the chin. I let gravity do its thing and fell, pulling him down with me.

The floor was flat again. They must have stabilized it. The Rider across from me shot his eyes at his prize and back at me, his obstacle.

"You won't stop us," he cursed.

"You're wrong."

He darted toward the Cerebrander. I could feel heat behind me. Redmond was defending my back. I shot forward, wrapped my whole body around the Rider, and started to freeze him.

"Oh, no you don't, you freak," he said, pushing a button on his belt that crisscrossed around his massive chest. After all this time, I had forgotten about the Riders' impressive hardware.

All across his chest, metal popped out. I had to let go as planes and valleys of metal shot out under my nose. He had a second skin of pure metal, and my ice couldn't hurt him.

I still threw ice all around him, freezing him in place. I ran across the Cerebrander and started hooking up all the doodads again. I tried to, anyway. I had no idea how it worked.

Something picked me up from behind.

"You're cute," a metallic voice sneered. His only communication came through his protection. He held me by the neck as I kicked wildly in the air. "La'R-Gon wanted me to get the Cerebrander and get out again. That was my mission. But you hurt me. I will squash you first."

He threw me to the floor and slammed his metallic foot down as I rolled away. I wasn't slow these days. All around me, other Riders were retreating. They had the sense to get out of there. Redmond's fire seemed to come from the deepest pit of hell.

It roared through the ship, almost animalistic, reflecting against the silver walls. But he had his hands full.

There were so many Riders. No wonder they won before.

But they wouldn't now.

I threw up an ice shield as the Rider brought his heavy metallic boot down. I had no time to get out of his way this time. He ground against my ice. I could hear it groaning.

I had no abilities here, not against the floor. I needed to copy the opposition. I had way too much riding on this. It wasn't just my life. It was all of them.

Redmond had done it before, turned completely fiery. A man made of flames. Natalie had become a full woman of ice. But I had lived a lot longer than both of them put together.

How did they do it?

My ice shield started breaking.

"Just a little bit more," the Rider teased. "I knew this would be just a quick grab and run. No one will fight me except a little stupid Burner. You're pretty, though. If you just surrender, you can come with me."

I stalled for time. I felt out through my body. Nothing gave me any clue on how to transform.

"Where are you going? What could I offer you?"

"Once I get off this ship, I've gotta contact La'R-Gon."

"He's not even here?" I demanded.

"Nope. I'm pretty sure he won't be a leader for much longer. He's shown weakness. So, will you succumb? Your skin would be nice to the touch if you turned off your ice. I've never had a Burner before. Humans, yeah. But Burners are…scary."

He thought I was listening to him, scared because we

were losing. But Redmond's fire was as emotive as his face. He was winning. Just a few minutes more and…

Minutes! How long had it been? I had lost track of time. I thought we were in the homestretch.

"You're too quiet," the Rider said. "The only way a Burner is quiet is when they're up to something."

"You're smarter than you look," I said, snapping myself to full ice and pushing his boot off me. He staggered but surprised me by staying upright. I couldn't see myself. I didn't even know what I had done. But judging by the Rider's surprise, I had done it.

Done what? I had no clue. I wanted to be fully ice. Now, I was. An ice person instead of just an ice controller.

"Please!" the Rider screamed and fell to his knees. I should have just run forward and smashed his body, crushing him with my ice form. But I hesitated. He was begging. I had never known a Rider to beg. "Don't kill me. La'R-Gon scares me. We're not all as bad as he is. He threatened my family."

The battle was ending. The ship shuddered a few times, but it stopped. I looked at the pathetic Rider.

"You don't know how bad it is. Only a few females are born in every generation. And even then, we're defenseless. We can only turn to others' skins to save us. Don't begrudge us that."

It was over. I had no reason to murder him. I had to destroy the mothership with the Cerebrander. But I'd have enough blood on my hands to save my future.

There had been no time to think about the Riders—the Imposters. I only had Rust's point of view. The ending of my world. Was it La'R-Gon that had done all this?

"Maybe we can have a discussion."

The fires started dying down. I turned to look at

Redmond across the way, too far away from me. It was over. I just had to get to the Cerebrander.

I looked back toward the Rider, but…

He was gone!

I looked over to the Cerebrander, and he had pulled it out again. And then he was out the door. It had only taken less than a second to lose everything.

He had been lying to me. All he needed was for me to lower my guard for an instant.

Redmond ran up to me, not as concerned with the stolen item. I melted back to myself. It was over. My act of mercy had been my last.

"Laoni! What is it?" Redmond said.

"He took it. I forgot this was war. You don't give quarter in war, or you lose. I've lost."

"Never." Redmond grabbed my hand and started running toward the door. I had no choice but to be pulled along with him. "Whatever is happening, it's not over yet. I just know it. And you're still here."

I blinked as three shutter doors opened and Redmond's warm hand pulled me along. "You do know…"

"I guessed," he said firmly. "Whatever the problem was, we're safe."

I couldn't believe it! He knew. I had been right. Mond had been alive in the future, so he could know without ruining anything.

"Yay," I whispered.

"I figure if you're still here, there's still time."

Time! Yes. There was. I wasn't back in the future yet. If the ship was still intact, whatever battle had happened out there was over. The Rider had no way off the ship!

I ran faster than ever. This time I was pulling Redmond along.

I saw the tail end of the Rider, holding the Cerebrander

over his head. He was still in his suit. He looked back, growled, and pushed himself faster.

It was a race then.

A race to save the future.

As we rounded the corner, Redmond cursed. "He's heading toward the escape pods. There are sixty of them. As you know, they are able to fly on their own. He'll take it and go..."

I knew in an instant. That Rider had talked way too much for his own good. He needed to contact La'R-Gon. He couldn't return to the ship that had brought him. I had seen Natalie in battle. Given any chance, she would have shot that ship out of the sky as soon as possible. This Rider had nowhere to escape to.

"There is only one place I know of that the Rider would go. The New York facility. That's where Paul had to go to contact anyone."

We rushed under shiny crisscrossed beams and through more doors. But it was too late. The Rider knew how to operate technology. He was already gone, the Cerebrander in tow.

"Get in," Redmond said. He opened a hatch that led to a tiny cabin, just big enough for three people, and I didn't question him.

I smashed a big red circle, hoping it was the ignition. My luck held. The ship's engines hummed to life. A viewscreen melted from the front's white walls. Seatbelts caught hold of us and pressed us against the seats. A round steering wheel grew from the middle and reached my hands.

"Hold on," I said, pushing the pedal down near my foot. I was so glad that Redmond had given me driving lessons once.

As a round opening showed the blue sky, I realized this was a bit different than wheels on the ground.

It was magnificent!

I sped across clouds. Around me, I saw burning debris. A huge ship, but not as big as the fathership or, presumably, the mothership, was spiraling down, going in and out of visibility. It was headed for the ocean. That's where we were now.

It was amazing to me how much La'R-Gon wanted the Cerebrander back. He was willing to risk the mothers that would help bring their kind to life. He was desperate.

Too bad for him, so was I.

Natalie's ship was unseen, back to being invisible. Within seconds, I spotted our enemy and followed him. He sped along until he angled his ship downward. The escape pods weren't equipped with invisibility, probably because they were so small, they could easily look like an airplane or a satellite.

The Rider had a good lead on us. And he only went faster. I had no idea why, as much as I had the pedal to the metal, our ship was lagging behind. There were so many doodads on the console. I hit one by one, seeing what happened.

I was grateful for the voice that came with each one.

"Oxygen on."

"Don't need that," I said.

"Altitude raised."

"Uh, no!"

Redmond helped and slapped a few buttons.

"Viewport opened."

"Carbon evacuated."

And all the while, the Rider's ship was getting further and further away.

I saw a silver button overhead and touched it.

"Turbo engaged. Top speeds can reach light."

"That's what I'm talking about!" I yelled and clutched

Mond's hand. He cackled and watched the very tiny ship get bigger and bigger.

"Let me drive," he begged.

It was no time for levity. But somehow, I had to laugh. Like Redmond said, this could be bad or good. Let's just have a great attitude!

"Next time," I said. "I'm enjoying myself way too much." I spun the wheel and headed downward. We were moving so fast, I barely saw when ocean became land and then buildings shot up.

"Oops, too fast," I said as we overshot the ship and New York completely.

Within seconds though, we were back.

"Watch it!"

I didn't even think. I just spun the wheel and turned over completely. I could see the ground was up now.

"He's firing at us," Mond said. "Good reflexes."

I pressed a green button that was green.

"Weapons mode engaged."

"Oh yeah!" Redmond said as a helmet lowered over his eyes and what looked like a video game controller stuck out of the passenger seat's console.

He grabbed it eagerly. I only saw red flashes of light slamming through the sky. I dodged as more came at us. I zoomed left and right as Redmond fired.

"Keep it steady, Laoni. I'm losing my target."

"He's trying to shoot us down!" I yelled. Far up above the buildings, where no one could see, an epic battle was happening.

Finally...

"Direct hit! That's all, you jackass!"

I laughed as the ship in front of us went down. "I'm beginning to think the two of us can do anything," I said as I followed the spiraling, smoking ship.

"Oh, wait!" Redmond said and pressed yet another button.

"Suspension hook activated. Aim with weaponry."

"User-friendly, isn't it?" I asked.

Redmond had already aimed the large metal hook like a fishing rod and reeled the ship in.

"No!" I screamed. Someone was jumping ship. Two parachutes. One was the Rider. The other was the Cerebrander.

"He keeps going and going…" Redmond said.

He wasn't worried. He had no idea there was a time limit on this.

I flew the ship down, dragging the other one along with us. I had to find a place to land. Unfortunately, the Rider had no such concerns.

Time was running out. I had to get to the Rider before he communicated with the mothership. From experience, I knew La'R-Gon could get there only minutes after someone called him.

That meant La'R-Gon would have the Cerebrander again. I wouldn't be able to do my burnout. And he'd have the Breathers again.

All of them were on the ship. It would truly all be over then.

"No defeatist thinking," Redmond reminded as we landed. "We'll survive. We always do."

But he was wrong. He didn't. Only I did.

I couldn't go through it again.

We jumped out of the ship and headed toward the building. We weren't far away. I ignored the humans around who saw our landing and gaped at us like we were creatures from another planet. They were wrong. That was the Riders.

This time, I'd kill him.

I couldn't lose.

I wouldn't.

CHAPTER 34

The facility looked the same, still as rundown as ever. We looked up and down as we entered, trying to find our prey. There! The Rider was kneeling with the Cerebrander on the floor beside him. He had one of the panels off the nearest wall and was creating a makeshift communicator.

Not for long!

I iced over the wall. He looked over his shoulder and cursed.

"Here's the deal," I said. I squeezed the air, making many icicles pop out of my hands and hover in the air. "I will kill you. Or you can give us the Cerebrander and run. How's that for you?"

The Rider snarled and jumped up into the air. He still wore his suit. Like Molly, his was as deadly. He straightened his arm and pointed his wrist. Two missiles exploded toward us.

Redmond cocked his head. "You are a real idiot. When fire meets missile, it goes boom."

The Rider snarled and spun in the air. Three more missiles exploded.

And as I expected, while Redmond destroyed those, the Rider disappeared downward—with the Cerebrander. Why did it have to be so portable?

"He'll do anything to distract us. He's trying to find another place he can communicate." I ran after the Rider.

The long staircase inside a narrow room was covered in debris.

"He works fast, I'll give him that," Redmond said. Funny, he didn't sound as hopeful as before.

This stuff was getting to him. I guessed it was my turn. "We'll make it. He doesn't have time to drop a line to La'R-Gon."

Redmond grimaced and sent fire down the stairs, burning everything in our way to a crisp. "That's not what I'm worried about. You are vulnerable down there. Still recovering. If you were a psychic manifestation, that'd kill you. Since you..." We climbed down the stairs slowly, watching out for anything the Rider could throw at us.

"Since you are a time traveler," he continued, but I saw he was a bit paranoid. He was getting the point of what the older Redmond figured out. "Then this, too, will end everything. When Paul saw you so weak and helpless, he completely changed. This Rider doesn't have dual sides. We can't let him hurt you."

I wasn't worried. All my goals were simple. Stop the Rider. Get the Cerebrander hooked up again. Burn out La'R-Gon's ship and people. I wasn't concerned with my future, but I should have known Redmond would be.

That was our thing. I worried more about him. He worried more about me.

"You keep an eye on me, then. I'll handle the Rider."

Redmond smiled. We reached the bottom of the staircase.

The door was closed. My heart started beating again. I had left it behind for so long. But Redmond reminded me to feel. That came with fear. I couldn't be happy and be me without also being afraid. It came as a packaged deal.

"This time, no mercy," I said. Without any more words, I wound up my arm like a pitcher and exploded the door, throwing it off its hinges and across the room.

The Rider was staring at me, suspended in the liquid. There was a sense of awe on his face. He looked back at me, then at the other Laoni, and grinned.

"Please, don't hurt me," he mocked. Then he laughed. "Oh, I guess that whining stuff won't work again. It shouldn't have in the first place. Useless, weak hearts. You are why we Dedgarnons are the superior species. We will be victorious." He looked at the Augmenter again. "Something tells me, pretty, that if I kill you in here, I'll kill her there, too," he said with a sick grin. His eyes roved my body and then took in the other one. "But the idea of having two of you does have its merits."

"Watch your mouth, or I'll burn your lips off," Redmond said. "You won't touch either one."

The Rider grinned and aimed his hand again, but this time, he pointed toward the ceiling right above my other self.

"No!" Redmond said, rushing forward. All of his fire did nothing. He tackled the Rider as he let off one of his missiles.

The world exploded around us. I raised my palm to the ceiling and protected myself in the liquid with a thin ice shield. It covered me as the roof collapsed. I heard a rumbling and remembered we were at the bottom of this place. The Rider had just collapsed a support beam.

"Hold it up, Laoni!" Redmond begged as he turned the Rider over on his stomach and wrenched his metal hands behind him.

"You'll never make it," the Rider said. "I am equipped with a self-destruct sequence. Suicide for me, but victory for my people. Too bad for the weak-skinned ones."

"You're ones to talk," I said. I felt the pressure of the building as I pushed more ice up to hold it in place. If the Rider did one more hit, I'd go down. We all would. "You steal other creatures' bodies. You are weak little slimy beings without your stolen bodies."

The Rider glared at me. Ah, I'd struck a nerve. Well, as long as I was at it. "Look at you. Couldn't hold onto one planet. Were you there when Simrul exploded? Did you watch as your incubators were destroyed and all your young killed too?"

The Rider was quivering. "You… How do you know about my world?"

That was the last straw! "It wasn't *your* world. It was the Simrulians'! They destroyed it to get you out. Now that I've seen your evil, I know why. I've encountered a few of your Dedgarnons. I knew them first as Breathers. But all of you are such…whiners!"

Great, as long as I was pissing him off, he wasn't doing his self-destruct. He wanted me dead. And as I suspected, I was making him so angry, he wanted to be the one to end my life.

"You are ours," he hissed, sounding like a snake. "You have no rights except to serve us. No being in the universe should be allowed to fight us. You should consider it an honor. An honor to be ours. To serve us!"

"Spoken like any true loser who tries to take over," I said. Everything was bubbling in my head. All my experiences. The path I'd taken. All to come here with a Rider at my mercy.

"Die," I said and sent an icicle into his head.

Whatever defense his suit had against the elements didn't

matter. Pure rage fueled my anger. The number of times I was helpless at the hands of either the Dedgarnons' creations or at their hands themselves. I had given this Rider a chance before, and it had almost destroyed everything.

Not this time.

The icicle burrowed into his body armor, and as I heard him scream, I knew it had hit his brain. As he quivered on the ground, the body armor disappeared, and the skin he wore shriveled up. The nasty creature that was left jiggled at our feet.

"Laoni! The ice!"

I shot my eyes upward and put out another sheet to catch the building as it tried to destroy us.

"No, no, no," Redmond moaned. I shook my head. I had it!

But then I noticed…the liquid was draining out of the Augmenter. A piece of debris had broken through. It had created a hole in my protection just like my icicle had drilled through the Rider's brain.

We had no choice. This place was going to go. "Get her. I mean, me. This place will collapse. I'll get the Cerebrander. I need to hook it up to the closest power source. Hopefully the whole building won't go down."

Redmond grabbed my arm and looked into my eyes. "No. If we take you out, you'll die."

I caressed his jaw. "If you leave me in there, I'll die. That liquid is almost gone. Look." I pointed out the fact that since the liquid no longer supported me, all the tubes and stuff that connected me to the Augmenter had been pulled out of my flesh. I was just sinking downward as the liquid left.

"Please, Mond. We don't have much time."

He groaned so deeply it hurt my heart and everything else inside me. But he ran across the room, gave one glance at the ice shield above him, and grabbed my unconscious body. I had to face it. I didn't look well. I… She still had long hair. It had not been cut by La'R-Gon, and it was purely black. Only a few strands of white. I was still worn out back in this time. Burned out.

I wouldn't last long. But it didn't matter right now!

"Come on!" I ordered. Redmond carried the unconscious me to the exit, and I grabbed the Cerebrander. What had I said about it being too bad it was so portable? Now, I was thrilled! We ran up the staircase, and I finally let the ice shield collapse. I crossed my fingers as the building shook, holding onto the fact that the whole thing couldn't come down.

And…I was right. As the tremors subsided, I gave a smile at Redmond.

"The panel that he opened. Can I use it to power the Cerebrander?"

Redmond nodded, but he was looking at the body in his arms. He knew she was doing badly.

"Talk me through setting it up, okay? We'll do it here."

"Do what? Save you?" he asked. His face was gray. Hope was draining out. He knew my answer.

"No. It won't save me."

"Then I don't care. Let the world burn. It doesn't deserve to exist if it kills someone like you."

I felt tears trickle down my cheeks. "I love you too, Mond. But our friends. You. They have a chance. You wouldn't let them die just for selfish reasons. And I won't let you."

"I want to be selfish! I can't lose you. I've lost you every single day since I left you. I can't do it again."

"Mond, I want to save people. You know that about me. Please, help me."

He looked at the body in his arms again, shifted his weight and held her tight. "Okay."

As I walked across to the panel and put the Cerebrander on the ground, I looked back at Mond. "It's not over. Hold me. Ask me not to leave you. I'll do anything for you. I might even survive."

He gave me a soulful look and pointed at the Cerebrander. "The blue wire goes into that one over there."

And we began.

Slowly but surely, we put the Cerebrander together. The process was slow, mind-numbing. I'd never liked this kind of thing. Mond was too busy holding my unresponsive body to do anything but direct me. But it worked. The panel was more than capable of hooking up the Cerebrander.

I didn't waste any time in putting the mask over my face. I even ignored that I could feel the worms now, burrowing into my pores, making connections with my brain.

I could hear Mond from across the way, begging my body to stay alive. "Stay with me, Oni. I love you. Don't leave. Survive. Live for us. We need to be together."

If anything could hold me there, it'd be Mond. He was the one who had saved me in the first place. Now, at the end, he would bring the beginning again. I smiled and reached out with my mind.

The world turned upside down. The past was left behind. I sat up, panicked. Rust was staring at me, his beard old and green. I was in the building Redmond had made, complete with all his inventions. There was no sign of old Redmond. No sign of anyone.

"You failed again?" Rust asked.

My mind exploded in pain and fear.

CHAPTER 35

ust asked again and again what was wrong. He didn't get it. No one would. I hadn't realized I was so close to running out of time. I had failed.

I felt myself rocking and crying more than anything else. I was outside time for a little longer, but sooner or later, everything would catch up to me. What had I done? I thought…

I cried more and more. I thought I was going to make it. I was so close. So much time wasted.

My breath still caught. My heart still beat. Why couldn't everything shut down with respect to the major blow I had just taken? I guessed soon, it would. But for the time being, I was still alive.

No one else was.

Well, except Rust. What I had done by releasing La'R-Gon had returned the timeline to what I knew. At least, it looked like it had.

I pushed myself into a corner and cried and heaved, then cried some more. My eyes were soggy lines. I could neither see nor hear Rust, who kept trying to help me eat or drink. I couldn't!

Let me die. Surely, Time wouldn't be so cruel to keep me out of time forever. Let me die!

"What happened?" Rust asked again as I took the cup of tea he was trying to get me to drink and threw it against the wall, watching the pieces slip down.

"I failed!" I cried. But it came out in a hoarse whisper. I had already ruined my throat. I couldn't even speak anymore through the tears. They were all gone. Redmond was gone.

"How, though?"

He was trying to get me to talk, to share, so that he could fix it. That was Rust.

I wouldn't answer.

He finally left me alone. I guessed it was night when he wrapped a blanket around me. "Get some sleep. We'll deal with whatever it is tomorrow."

How little he knew! I wouldn't tell him. Soon, he'd die too. He could discover on his own that there were no more chances.

I closed my eyes. The world inside melted. I didn't care to look. Time was bringing me forth.

"You cry now, do you?"

I blinked at the little geode, full of fathomless crystals. It was speaking to me. *"You should rejoice. You had a chance not many mortals get."*

"Send me back." It was all I could manage. "I didn't fix anything. All of it was useless."

"Your fault, not mine. I should have known I wouldn't even get gratitude."

"For what?" I demanded. Swirls of color released from my mind. Angry reds. Ribbons of ice and light, wrapping around Time and pushing back. "You gave me hope. But you took away more chances. I hate you for it!"

The geode slammed the colors back, grew into a mountain, spun in place, and became the cat again. *"You dare? I gave you powers beyond mortal limitations. You ripped a hole in my realm. It still is there, bleeding. You are back where you came from when you shouldn't be. The hole keeps you aware and alive. Upon returning, you should have dispersed into dust."*

I didn't care. But I had to ask. "Because I died, didn't I? I didn't finish my stay in the Augmenter. I died back then. In Redmond's arms."

Time wriggled and grew tails and legs. *"Yes. You did."*

"You brought me here to thank you. Okay, thank you. You've ruined my life. Thanks so much for giving me a chance that should never have been taken. Thanks for putting so many rules on me that I didn't have time to figure out how to fix it. I hate you! I *hate* you so very much."

I should have known sneering at almighty beings wouldn't be good, but I was beyond caring. For one second, and only one, I thought that Time would tell me I'd have another shot. That I'd be sent back to the beginning and have all this knowledge. But I didn't hope for long.

Life was over. My world was over.

I woke up on my side, still in the corner. Time wouldn't speak to me anymore. My time-traveling days were over. Maybe I could have gotten on Time's good side, but I didn't have it in me. Besides, I doubted it.

Rust came to me with breakfast. I ignored it and him.

"Laoni, I don't know what happened. I know you were dead. But I know our mission. Somehow, the past changed. We can change it again."

That was the thing, we couldn't.

"Look, let's just take the Journeyer and go talk to Time again."

"Go away! Leave me alone! Run outside and let the damned Neo Breathers kill you or Paul or whatever is alive out there! Just do it. There's nothing left. Don't you get that? Nothing! I want to be left here and wait for death. It's over!"

Rust's mouth gaped open and he lost his strength, staring at me. I had ripped his hope away. I never should have given it to him in the first place.

"But...Time has no barriers. You can't give up," Rust said, trying to keep going.

But it did have barriers. The Cerebrander was supposed to...

I froze. Little tendrils of hope wiggled in my head, coming from the razed ground. The Journeyer was still here. That meant Redmond hadn't died when I did. He had lived on. Even past my death? How could he?

Almost unbidden, his words came to me. "They say that time is relative. That things happen, and then they're gone. But it's not true." He had reminded me that I was living through so much pain, I was always there, and even the effects of time had no impact on that.

Redmond had believed in that. So, when I died, he kept going. He knew I had died. Unlike before, when I had only been trapped far away from him, he still continued on.

He had faith in me.

My mind...could transcend even time.

"No... It's not possible. Is it?" I asked Rust.

He gave me a look of pure despair. "I don't know."

I blinked. I had been trying to get to the Cerebrander to send a weapon across the mind. I was pretty sure I could do it because I had created my ice motorcycle and traveled to Time itself. Couldn't I destroy a ship?

I thought I could.

But...the mind is a funny place. It's not affected by time. Not really. I had proved that when I time-traveled with just my will. What had Time said about mortals' will? It can change the very fabric of space and time. But there was a caveat. Only if the being has a desire greater than one's own selfish wants and needs.

It was selfish to give up, only caring about my despair. I didn't even worry about what I was doing to Rust. Telling him to off himself, what kind of person was I? No, it wasn't over. I wouldn't let it be.

"Rust, I'm sorry. I…I won't give up. Neither can you. The Journeyer, is it working?"

Rust nodded. Light started shining from his face. To think I could have ripped it out so utterly. No. Not anymore.

I rushed back toward the Journeyer. It was in the same place as it was before.

"I'm not going to give up, Redmond. Never again!"

I slipped in and pulled the mask down. It felt warmer than the Cerebrander. More comfortable. Like home.

"Last chance," I said. This time, I felt no worms. A caress. Warm light.

I couldn't travel through time anymore. But by pure will, there was another way.

I closed my eyes and looked around the chaos, but I didn't wait long. I didn't need Time to get interested in what I was doing. I wasn't going to make the wound bigger. My body wouldn't step back in time at all. But my mind would.

With a whistle, I called forth my bike. It glowed with more fervor. See-through icy wheels. A handlebar of white ice. Tires of black. I slipped on and pulled Mond close.

"I won't give up."

And I searched. Where was the mothership? Not in this time. Nope. My body needed to stay put. My mind was limitless.

I roared backward. I wouldn't go forward. I spun the wheels on sewing buttons. The roar of my being filled my mind. But I kept going backward.

Images appeared in front of me, like I was driving down a highway. The billboards and signs were memories.

Rust was alone.

Years went back. Then he had some help, some friends. My friends.

There was Mond—at forty. He was looking insanely handsome. All tall and big-faced, a little beard skirting his cheeks. Yum, yum.

But I kept going backward. Starry skies fell to blue skies.

I saw everything and nothing.

Then I saw…

Central HQ. Halfway standing. Mond standing over my body.

"Sorry, Mond, but at least I'll save you."

Then I spun my wheels toward the sky, and I burst out… Wow!

I was over New York City. Okay, maybe I wasn't. My bike still hovered without any logic or gravity. The coordinates! I quickly remembered the coordinates Rust gave me. I had no other choice. I couldn't forget.

I had seen them in the stars, hidden from our sensors. Far beyond the moon, just sitting there, waiting for an attack. I drove my motorcycle to the ship. Invisible, but I could almost see it. It dwarfed me. A big silver bowling ball with flattened sides, an angry mouth that didn't speak. I felt like a speck against a sun.

But I wasn't here. My body was still far in the future where La'R-Gon won.

"La'R-Gon," I whispered. And bam. There I was. Roaring my motorcycle next to his chin. I still floated, but he had no idea I was there.

I only said one sentence. "Freeze, you misbegotten slimeball."

My ice exploded through the corridors. I saw La'R-Gon's face looking completely shocked as he turned into a statue.

I heard the screams of the Imposters. Throughout the ship, one by one, they froze. I flicked the ship's machinery. Suddenly, it was sent out of control.

Then I roared out of the ship, watching the nothing fall away. I could only see the edges. The invisibility was failing. I had frozen the entire ship.

I turned my wheel and rounded my hands. "Freeze, all of you. Every ship. Every last one of you." I didn't see the effects. I just knew. I had won. My motorcycle disappeared. I was pulled back through space and time.

I opened my eyes and saw Rust staring at me. "Did it work?" I wasn't sure. Had it all been in my mind? "What's your history?"

"The same thing that happened before. We all lost. There was..." He wrinkled his eyebrows. "No. There was no invasion. There was nothing. The Imposters all just disappeared. Nothing was left."

He blinked. "In fact, I can't remember why you went back in time. I can't remember anything..."

Suddenly I was on the floor. I was sitting on nothing but metal now. "What the? The Journeyer is gone!" I said. But that wasn't all. Rust looked down at his hands. In front of us both, they were going away. He was fading out of existence, piece by piece.

"What's happening?"

"You don't exist," I said with a smile. "Neither do I. We both died a long time ago."

"You did!" he agreed, watching his feet dissolve under him. "But I wouldn't. If everything's good, I still should live."

I shifted. "Okay, maybe not. But you don't belong here. Your history has changed. You succeeded. I killed La'R-Gon."

Rust's eyes brightening into suns was the last I saw of

him. The building rearranged around me. Lots of others grew up. This was the new future.

I kicked my legs out, only to see my feet were gone. So, the hole was closing. I no longer belonged here.

"Goodbye," I said out loud. I ignored the people coming to life. Bunches of workers. Businesspeople. Future technology. Everyone living their lives. No concern for me. Like a fuzzy old television, the world regained its focus. My eyes were losing color.

I was dead in the past. No one could save me. Now, I was rejoining myself.

The sun seemed cold. The world was empty. My arms went next. Then my torso. I was only a head. Then I was only my mind, reaching out to the past, holding on to Mond.

"Mond," I said though I didn't speak. "I'll always love you. Goodbye."

And I spun forever into nothingness.

I no longer existed. Time was somewhere laughing at me. I could no longer be here.

But I had succeeded. I didn't give up. I did what Mond had said. I kept the good possibility in my mind.

And that made all the difference.

CHAPTER 36

There were firm arms around me, holding me. I could hear his whisper. "Don't leave me, Laoni. Don't give up."

I knew who it was. It broke my heart to hear the pain in his voice. I had caused that pain.

I reached up and touched his lips. "Don't cry."

Mond gasped and touched my face. I wrenched my eyes open, staring at him. When did he get short hair? The last thing I remembered was…I was heading for Molly.

Then there was…

"Oni, can you move? Are you okay?"

I smiled. Somehow, I was. I didn't know how. I was dying. I was attacking the Imposters. No…

"Oni, speak to me. Come on. You're getting stronger. But I thought you were dying."

"Of course I was. Molly had to be stopped."

Mond moved a little and pulled on me. He wanted me to stand, to show my strength. But it was so nice to be curled up with him.

"Oni, please."

I gazed into his eyes. He had been through it, hadn't he? I needed to move, to show him I was okay. I felt better than ever. I jumped up, my ballgown rustling, and pulled him with me. "Hi," I said and kissed him, running my fingers through his short hair. I liked it like this, though I missed my fingers getting caught.

We didn't separate for a while, but finally, when we pulled apart, gasping for breath, Mond stared at me again. "Your hair…it's not mostly black. More like half and half."

"Your hair is short," I said and squeezed his hand. "What happened?"

"You…right. I have so much to tell you. But I've gotta know. Was she a psychic projection of you?"

I had to laugh. "Who?"

Mond swung my arm, but I had a chance to look around. This place was a mess. Half the building had collapsed around us. Some strange-looking machine was plugged in and humming, though an incessant beeping was aggravating my ears. Rubble was everywhere.

"This isn't the basement," I said, trying to puzzle it out. I remembered riding the ice motorcycle. No, that was a dream inside my Augmenter.

"It collapsed," Mond said. He wasn't looking at anything but me, his eyes hungrily searching for what, I couldn't tell. "The… A lot has happened. See, this Laoni from the future came back in time to save us all."

My eyes widened. I touched his lips and shushed him. "No…you can't. Everything will end."

Mond stared at me. "What?"

What indeed! I had no clue what I was talking about. I was filled with unbelievable paranoia about something that I didn't even know. "The future?" I tried. The fear lessened as I spoke. It wasn't real anymore, whatever I was scared about.

"Yes." Mond started to smile. "You can finally talk about it. Something changed. What's the last thing you remember?"

I closed my eyes. I saw so much. Old Rust. Strange buildings. Insanity rushing through half of my mind. "The last real thing was fighting Molly. Then I died. You caught me."

Mond shook his head and pulled on my hand. He wanted us out. I could see why.

"The Cerebrander," I said. "We can't just leave it. Even with La'R-Gon's death, it could be used against us."

Mond stared at me. "He's dead?"

"Yes." I stopped talking. I had no proof of that. Memories were fragmented inside my head. Half were gone. Half were there. I couldn't walk through it all. My head hurt.

"But…only the future Laoni could know that. She wasn't a psychic…?"

"No!" But I was laughing. "It was future Laoni. I seem to have dual memories. What happened while I was gone?"

Mond filled me in. As he did, we unhooked the Cerebrander and powered it down. I wanted to destroy it, but Mond shook his head.

"No. I kind of like the design. I think I could mimic it. Someday. And who knows what we could connect with."

I swallowed. Words came to my head. "I *hate* you so very much." But they gave me nothing but a flash of a cat with six tails and nine feet. Insanity.

"So, what do you think happened?" I asked as we walked out. "The future Laoni solved everything. But then, why do I have some of her memories? I mean, not all. But I've seen an older you. Somehow."

He gave me a grin. "Time isn't something I know anything about. But it sounds like an intriguing concept, to be able to control it."

We walked down the street, looking from left to right. Part of my brain told me that I had nothing to worry about.

But what I had last seen was Molly and a whole slew of Breathers and Riders who wanted us dead. I couldn't let my guard down. Not now, anyway.

"But I'd guess that somehow you and she united together. Like, two Laonis couldn't exist at the same time, no matter what. So, you are both."

I laughed long and hard. "That sounds like something out of a book. I don't…"

I trailed off as Mond led me to a spaceship. Not like the one that we destroyed, but a smaller one. All brown and round. With cannon barrels sticking out the front and a tail like a fish on the back. There was no way of seeing inside, but Mond acted as if he knew it was there.

"Um, that Laoni really did come back in time, didn't she?"

Mond pulled my hand so I could climb into the passenger seat. The seatbelts slapped around us. Why did this seem so familiar? But I had no memories.

"I wouldn't joke about this. Not when she…you saved our lives. All of us. If La'R-Gon is dead, we're free. We need to get back to the other ship."

It washed over me. Familiar, but so foreign. "Other ship?"

"Natalie's now. Thanks to you again."

I watched as Mond hit some buttons and easily turned the ship on. "I wonder if this thing could have invisibility. We were in the midst of a major battle before. So, we couldn't exactly check."

"It's probably too small," I argued. But I felt like a cloud was around me. My thoughts weren't mine. I should have been in awe of this ship. But I had been in it before. I had been flying it.

"I wonder." Mond touched a button under the seat. A computerized voice floated in.

"Reflection mode on."

"Aha! See how wrong you are," he teased.

Okay, so I was. Cool. We popped up into the sky. I took a long look at the abandoned building I had been in up to just a few minutes ago. It looked so benign from the outside. Whatever collapsed inside wasn't apparent. It looked like one of the many other buildings on this street. The people looked up at the sky but didn't see us.

"We won." I couldn't feel anything. There was something going on. We had more than won. Somehow, I had survived the future and still came back. "It was Time."

"What was?" Mond asked, holding my hand and kissing it as he focused on steering.

"I fell through a hole in time. I came back together with myself. She would have died. But somehow, someway, Time put me back. She joined me and her. That's how I'm alive."

Mond was quiet as we sped through the clouds. The ship detected a bird in our way and veered easily around it. I couldn't believe this was made by the Riders. Imposters. It cared about life. But maybe it hadn't been a product of the Riders. Maybe they had stolen it like they had stolen everything else. But they wouldn't anymore.

I had burned out every single Rider, whether on the surface or a ship. I had reached out with my mind and targeted each and every one of those evil creatures. And they all were evil. Memories were flowing in. At one point, I had hesitated when a Rider had begged for his life. I had thought it was all La'R-Gon's fault. Or Molly's. Molly had succumbed to evil, but the Imposters were a disease that destroyed anything that got in its way.

I had read Rust's diaries in the future. Faded memories. When Mond was… I couldn't remember. But Rust had talked about his pain, the loss of his world.

Finally, I had avenged him.

"But…" Mond broke me out of my reverie. "You're not back. Your hair is half white, half black. And your powers?"

I turned my palm up and created a bust of my favorite face in the world. Mond's icy eyes stared at me, warm as the sun. "I still got it."

He collapsed in relief. I could hear a sob in his throat. This had hurt him. I put the miniature bust on the ship's dashboard and held him. I put my face in the crook of his neck, breathing him in.

I had no firm memories from the other me. Or me in the future. But I knew enough. I had sacrificed everything to save everyone.

The little ship skimmed the sky and Mond looked around the emptiness. "It should be right there."

"Host Ship recognized. Docking will initiate in ten seconds. Nine, eight, seven..."

"Man, I love this ship. I wonder if Natalie will let me keep it," Mond said.

I jiggled his arm. "Hey, I was the one who drove it first. I've got first dibs."

He gave me a grin and pulled me closer. "I'll persuade you."

With a gentle kiss on my chin, on my cheeks, we held each other while the little ship docked on its own.

~*~

It took a while to gather everyone up. I thought it best for this announcement to be huge, and to not have to say it again and again a hundred times. Everyone was still in the process of repairing the ship and wondering what had happened to the Riders in the jail. Their skins had shriveled up and only their decaying alien monster forms were stinking up the place.

Natalie waved for everyone to quiet. We were in the main part of the ship, where all the elevators and corridors ended. It was big and silver, but my friends had already taken it over. Cindy loved art and painted some cool characters on the walls. I was chagrined to see myself in one of them, looking fiercer than I ever could, my hair billowing out around me.

Erin had put many throw pillows, rugs, and beanbag chairs around, so it looked like a college dorm more than a spaceship. Bobby still loved bugs, but in respect to the rest of us who got the creeps from them, he had instead added his touch by having a dozen or so different kinds of flying machines hanging down, along with tanks, Jeeps, and Ferraris on shelves.

Funny. They had only had this ship briefly, but they were making it home. I knew why too. They never had a permanent home. They had to make do with what they had and feel at home even when they weren't. For many, the facility I grew up in was a second home. Then the island. Now the ship.

I couldn't wait to tell them they were free. This wasn't home, just really cool spoils. My memory was wonky, but I knew this ship was the last one on Earth. And it was ours.

"Okay, everyone," I said, looking around at all of them. Natalie was sitting in a soft chair. Cindy was splayed out in a beanbag chair. Bobby sat on a red divan. I stood on a circular rug to address them. "Hi. Hi. I love all of you."

Erin groaned and rolled her eyes. Cindy just grinned.

"Love ya back," Bobby said. "Nice announcement. I've got things to do." He stood up as if to leave.

"Bob, could you just stay put?" I said. "That wasn't the announcement."

I stared them all in the face and tears formed in my eyes. "We're free. We're Burners. But now we control where we go. Our enemies are dead. We all have a choice."

And we did.

CHAPTER 37

LAONI

Diary,

Today, I woke up to the sun smiling through my window. Yes, my window. Well, it's a window in my mother's house. But she says it's my room. For once, I believe her. When I went to pick up Mom from the island, she hugged me so tight, I was afraid I might ice-burn her again. But I didn't.

Everyone is so happy. I can still hear the screams of joy echoing in my ears when my friends actually believed me. At first, they thought I was pulling their legs. As if I would!

Mom and Drake are almost annoyingly supportive of me. It was refreshing today when Mom snapped at me to clean my gosh-darned ice sculpture up after I was done. So normal!

We're settling into the amazing house. I'm home.

The first few nights were hard. I didn't like being away from everyone, and I kept expecting a Breather attack. Oh, the Breathers! Update on them. I made peace with Paul. He was the only one still alive in the prison of the ship.

I'd had more than enough to be magnanimous. I apologized for what I did. He had a lot of time to think it over. Watching the crea-

ture he had shared a cell with explode had helped to convince him those monsters needed to be stopped, no matter the cost.

He forgave me. I guess he, too, had enough in him. After all, it was over.

It's over! I'm still reeling from that. All the surviving Breathers are slipping into their own homes, making lives. Paul agreed to be the go-between with all the legal stuff so Breathers could become part of any community they'd like.

Drake, too, is helping the crossover. Many Breathers already had homes, readying for an invasion that I stymied. The others listened to Natalie when she told them it was best to go on with their short lives. They don't have much living to do. I think even Paul is okay with his mortality now because he can relax. And no Neo Breathers are around for him to use. So, all's well that ends well.

Oops, I gotta go. Mom's calling for me. She says there's a vampire at my door.

Is this thing ever going to be over?

I don't mind.

Life is good.

EPILOGUE

he vampire was Lev. He was just giving me an update after giving one to Natalie. I supposed he thought we were the new game in town. Or that message I sent out through the… Uh, I'm still a little foggy on that part. I remember making the Breathers love all Burners. For some reason, my message also applied to the more supernatural kind.

That whole thing had me on edge a bit, but not too much. My whole life had been lived on the edge of a knife. An edge of a table wasn't bad. Still, it was never comfortable when a whole group of Breathers loved you on general principle. But, I guess, it was way better than hating you and wanting to rip you apart.

Mom came into my room with a lot of paperwork, but she smiled and sat beside me. "It's good to have you home. I…"

I knew what she wasn't saying. "They're my friends, Mom. All of them. I wouldn't be able to live here if they were far away."

"But is there really an alien ship hovering over my

house?"

There was. Natalie and the others all voted that the alien ship would be their second home for the time being, while everything was settled on the ground. There was so much to be done now. All the Burners had families. Cindy especially wanted to get in touch with hers. Some had been, of course, bought and paid for, so they were just going to stay on the ship for as long as it took them to grow up.

But some were going to college.

"Yes, it's our spoils." I gave a shaky grin as, once again, she drew me in. Mom was sure touchy-feely. I was so not used to it. My powers were back. The ones that could still freeze her if I didn't wear the special clothing.

Gone were my amazing powers from the future. I had only been given the strength to survive. I still felt a little off about that. I couldn't have survived without Time helping me. But why? Did it feel sorry for me? I don't believe that's a possibility. Was there something more Time had in mind, something that I had to do and wouldn't work if I had died? Who knew? I tried not to think about it.

"Mom, this is my home now. But it's not Redmond's. And where he goes, I follow."

Mom scoffed as she had done every single time I told her how serious it was between us. She didn't know. I had lived a lifetime with him—in a way. I knew what his future self would be. And I wouldn't change anything about what I was doing now.

"There are a lot of guys in college," she teased.

I rolled my eyes for two reasons. One, because she didn't see what I did when I talked about Redmond. And two, because I was still on the fence about going to college. "I've never been to school," I reminded her. "Why start now?"

Her face crumpled. I had asked the wrong thing. "Because I missed it all! Okay? Because I traded your life away and never got the chance to see you on your first day of high school. Heck, I didn't even see you enter second grade. I lost all of it. Everything. But the danger's over now, right?"

The room seemed small. I could smell the rosemary that Drake was using on the chicken downstairs. The tree outside scratched my window. And just beyond that, hovering, was the misshaped air that hid an invisible ship.

Everything *was* over. Why shouldn't I move on?

"I guess. But I don't know what to do."

Mom cheered up. She bounced my flowered quilt as she launched off my bed to grab the papers she had brought in. "GED applications. After that, applications for the community college not far from here."

My eyebrows rose. "Not far?"

"Hey, I saw you and Redmond zipping around in that 'car' of yours—a spaceship. Don't let Gem see you, by the way. She worships you. She'll want a turn!"

I laughed. I squashed my toes into my thick carpet and pulled the papers into my lap. "Hey, wait! This is an application to the University of California!"

Mom spread her hands and danced a little around the room. "They have one of the best art programs. You could get in. With your accomplishments…"

I just stared at her. I didn't know what to say.

Mom watched my face for a minute and gave me a secret grin. "They aren't just a hobby. I snuck a peek at your line of ice sculptures. You're hiding them in the forest, but I…"

My jaw dropped. "You've been following me?" I demanded.

"Just sometimes! I don't want you out of my sight. Anything could happen."

I didn't remind her that everything had. I wasn't sure if I wanted to get mad at her for invading my privacy or be touched that she knew what my sculptures meant.

I decided to tackle another issue. "Mom, you know that Burners are still a secret. We can't go and tell everyone—for many different reasons."

Mom pursed her lips and spread the papers on my bed. "That could be debated."

"No! For one, we are just getting used to no longer running from the Breathers. Two, who knows how many more out there might want to exploit our gifts? The Riders are gone, but the humans who allied with them? We have no clue where they are or how many there are. They know our bodies create an exceptional amount of energy. Then, there are the others."

Mom shushed me. "Okay, I didn't say I would debate it. I just think it could be. Besides, I'm talking about your strength and decorum. You're smart, think on your feet, and are very creative. You'd be an asset to any college. We can argue about that later. You still need a GED and more schooling before taking on a university. That's in the future."

I gave her a smile and did what she wanted. I filled out all the forms minus the Californian one. I wasn't so sure I even fit into college. I had to check and see.

When I was done, I went down to dinner. All my friends had been invited. I sat next to Redmond, and Erin and yelled at Cindy to pass the potatoes. We could have had this dinner in a much bigger area, but Mom and Drake didn't like the ship and refused to board it.

Gem pointed toward her soda, and I flicked some coldness at it. She watched in awe. I loved that look. It was much nicer than the fear she had when we first met.

As lots of conversations broke out, Erin looked at the table. She wasn't all that happy. I couldn't blame her. Her parents had been killed...recently? I was still a bit messed up by all the time travel. I was from the future, but I was still present-day Laoni.

"You okay?" I asked her.

"Everything's back to normal," she said. "But is it? I need to find a way to live normally. Now that's scary. I don't want to talk about it."

I listened. There was too much food to talk through anyway. This was the first celebration we had together. Drake had stopped at nothing. Big chickens and hams were on the table, surrounded by mountains of side dishes. Fruit pies were for dessert, along with a strange kind of really strong tea, but I liked it.

I sat back and looked at all my friends. My family.

This was what I had been fighting for. This normal moment. Redmond had a smear of gravy on his cheek that I wanted to lick off. Cindy was holding Erin's hand to help her relax into the moment. The light in her eyes was shining more than ever before. Her parents would accept her back, I just knew it. And unlike Erin's, they wouldn't have to fear.

No one did anymore.

We had won.

After dinner, Redmond and I went on a walk. He knew I loved making ice sculptures every night, and lucky for us, neither of us got cold. But I had to warn Redmond we had to be careful with Mom sneaking around the woods after us.

"I like the squirrel," Redmond noted as we came to the end of my sculptures. I had asked him not to look until I was finished, but I had just done that cutey last night. A squirrel had been on the branch watching me. It stayed still enough for me to make a copy of it. But I had used a lot of shaded ice in it. It was incredible how much I could do. I wondered what my true limits were. No matter how long I had been enhanced in the Augmenter, I hadn't matured. I hadn't reached my full potential.

Only time would tell how much more powerful I could get. Only Natalie might know, but she and her sister had been holding back their powers for years. I was the first true Ice Burner to show what our powers could be.

"Do you think Nora misses the island?" Redmond asked. I was starting a new sculpture. It was of Redmond. I had waited for him because my mind had been in a place of turmoil since everything had ended. I was finally starting to relax.

I shook my head. "No, she really doesn't. I mean, any time she wants to, she can grab an escape pod and go back if she wants. She missed her sister, and they're together again. Everyone is. The island is for vacations and that's it. Erin is going back because her siblings are still there."

Mond leaned against a tree, watching me pull my fingers and spin ice. "How's it going with them? They still aren't quite there."

I nodded. "I know. But…the Cerebrander is shut down. The Flyers are making sure all the computers that are attached to them are destroyed. There's a whole lot of clean-up to be done. I…"

Mond quickly shushed me. "No. Oni, you've done enough. You are done. Okay? Now the only thing you have to do…the only thing *we* have to do is continue like we should have when we were young. I am going to look up my family soon. You have yours. Let's try and be normal, okay?"

I looked at him and gave a grin. I wouldn't tell him that I had a strange feeling life, at least mine, wasn't that simple. There was more out there. More to be done.

But for now, I finished my sculpture, and we walked out of the forest. Overhead, I saw escape pods leap out of the invisible air and become invisible themselves as their drivers headed wherever they wanted to go.

This was my home and our new home base. No need for running.

We all burned in the same area now.

There were still things to be done. Erin and her siblings were a reminder that the Imposters' scars still showed. The Breathers weren't perfect, and that feeling of evil might have gone deep. All my friends had to look up family members and see if they still wanted them.

And then there was the dreaded school where I might have to...where we *all* might have to hang around normal people for a change.

All of that was ridiculous, insane, absolutely terrifying— if I wasn't already terrified out.

But for now, I was at peace. I leaned against Redmond's chest as his arms encircled me. We watched the moon rise, spilling its light against the peaceful sky, and beyond that, the peaceful solar system.

The Imposters were dead.

Our lives could continue.

Redmond and I burned against each other the rest of the night.

ABOUT THE AUTHOR

Marianna Palmer is a creative force who has been crafting captivating stories from the depths of her imagination since she first learned to dream. Encouraged by a dare from her sister, she bravely embarked on a journey into the world of writing, which became her sanctuary during years of solitude, personal challenges, and overcoming deep-rooted fears.

With an unwavering passion for storytelling, Marianna pursued her education and proudly earned her BA degree. However, she didn't stop there. Preferring the enigmatic allure of privacy, she briefly disappeared from the public eye, resurfacing intermittently in the company of her sister before once again retreating into her world of words.

Currently residing in the vibrant city of Tacoma, WA, Marianna draws inspiration from the beauty of her surroundings while reveling in the safety of her sister's presence. Determined to live life to the fullest, she fearlessly confronts the unknown, defying the daunting obstacles that once hindered her path.

https://mariannapalmer.wixsite.com/website

twitter.com/MariannaPalme18
instagram.com/mariannapalmerauthor
tiktok.com/@mpalmerwrites
bookbub.com/authors/marianna-palmer

ABOUT THE PUBLISHER

VISIT OUR WEBSITE
TO SEE ALL OF OUR HIGH QUALITY BOOKS:

http://www.redempresspublishing.com

Quality trade paperbacks, downloads, audio books, and books in foreign languages in genres such as historical, romance, mystery, and fantasy.

www.ingramcontent.com/pod-product-compliance
Lightning Source LLC
Chambersburg PA
CBHW020105310726
48970CB00002B/483